Ga … tales

nurturing
children's wellbeing
through stories.

Martha Begley Schade

Martha Begley Schade, Galway, Ireland

Illustrated edition published in Ireland in 2020

Title: Galway Fairytales Merlin Woods Series

This book is a work of fiction and tells the stories of various wood animals who all deal with different social issues such as bullying, friendship, kindness, teamwork, homelessness and depression.

Registered with Nielsen Pubeasy where you can order this book or, alternatively, you can contact the author herself at **marthabegleybooks@gmail.com**.

Illustration work was done by Nicolae I. Nistor

Cover Design is by Stuart McNeill from LRS Animation

First Edition.

ISBN 978-1-9162122-6-8

Contents

About the Author

Martha Begley Schade is a writer and author of the highly acclaimed Galway Fairytales – Merlin Woods series.

After years of working in business management, during which she had also written several books relative to her work, she has now put pen to paper to realize a lifelong dream of story-telling, a talent that was handed down through generations in her family.

With a B.Sc. in physics & maths, and an MBA, her new venture into children's storytelling comes from a lifelong passion of entertaining and educating children.

After 22 great years of living and working in Germany, she returned to Galway in 2008 with her two sons. The only place she ever wanted to live, she finds the Tribes people are the kindest and most caring she has ever met.

Together with the sea air, the seagulls flying overhead, the buzz of the city, the glistening beaches and beautiful hills of Connemara, all combine to only cement her love for her adopted home.

Flappy

The Pigeon Who Overcame Bullying
From zero to hero

Introduction

What I am about to tell you shouldn't really have become a famous story .... but such is life. Fame and fortune can come from the strangest of places or have the oddest of reasons!

You see, once upon a time in the West of Ireland, in a place called the Merlin Woods in Galway, a pigeon mother was sitting on her nest high up in a tree. She was about to hatch out six of the cutest little chicks you have ever seen! The following story I am told is true, as true as I am sitting here telling you this: it is about one of those little chicks that was hatched on that now famous day.

The Story

It was a bright sunny morning in late spring. The sun's rays flickered through the leaves in the wood and a gentle breeze rustled through the lush green leaves, making them shiver and dance.

The chicks had just hatched and proud Momma pigeon eagerly checked out her newly hatched squabs with pride. They were all just so pretty and so delicate. They would need a lot of care and special milk, she thought to herself – and Poppa Pigeon would have to help out with that too.

She chuckled to herself and her heart swelled with happiness as she spread her wings widely to blanket over her newborns.

Happily, she settled down to rest with them for a while – until the next feeding time. That would be very soon again, she groaned. These were very hungry chicks who needed so much food to grow big and strong.

And so it was that over the next few days and weeks the proud parents took turns. While one kept sentry, the other went off to look for more and still more food.

After only four days the chicks had opened their eyes to see the world for the very first time! They got bigger and stronger every passing day, and their chirpings rang out loud and clear in anticipation of their next meal.

Learning to Fly

Soon the day came when it was time for the fledglings to make their first attempt at leaving the nest. Momma Pigeon clucked worriedly around her babies, giving orders, warning them not to go too far and to strictly follow her instructions.

She moved over to sit at the edge of the nest and, ordering all six to line up behind her, spread her wings and leapt into the wide-open air.

Flapping her wings to gain a little height, she then sailed gracefully to the ground nearby.

Tweeting loudly, she called on her babies to follow her. She sang to them. Cajoling. Encouraging them to take the first step outside their nest into the big wide world.

It was their turn now, like their Momma and Poppa, indeed just like all pigeons that had ever gone before them. First came the strongest. Now he fluffed out his wings, ruffled his feathers, gave a confident leap into the air and started to flap his wings. And what do you know? He was flying. He took to it like a duck to water. He was a true natural, so good that he even landed fairly close to his Momma.

The next chick was watching this closely. She was thinking to herself: "Well, if he can do it, so can I!" She quickly followed suit and also landed not so very far away from her anxious Momma.

And so it was that one by one they all stepped up to the edge of the nest, spread out their young and eager wings, took a leap into the great unknown, flapped their wings and sailed down to where the ever-happier Momma was waiting.

That is all of them except the last little one. But why? Because he was always just that little bit different from the others. Somehow he was not as graceful or dainty as they were.

His Momma and Poppa had even decided to give him a special name: "Brian", which means "the one with strength and vigour". They wanted him to feel strong and not like a weakling (that they secretly feared he might be).

Brian climbed to the edge of the nest. Balancing unsteadily on the spot, he ruffled his feathers, spread out his wings and, taking the strongest jump he could manage, left the nest. Oh my word, was he nervous! He felt the wind blowing in the outside world for the first time. It tickled his feathers and with that, he spread out his wings even further.

At that point, everyone gasped. His Momma. His Poppa, and all that had come to watch from the other trees or on the other branches. They all gasped in astonishment.

"Look!", they cried. "Look at his wings!"

As Brian spread his wings everyone saw for the very first time that Brian had the most enormously long wings for such a small pigeon.

Of course Brian didn't realise this. He was concentrating on flying for the first time. His wings had always been this size - well, for the last four weeks anyway. He was far too busy anyway to notice the shock on the other pigeons' faces. So he raised his wings high. Then he beat them downwards. He could feel his body beginning to soar, taking him to new heights. His natural instinct soon had him swinging them back up towards the sky.

That was the moment when what happened next happened for the very first time!

Now please don't get me wrong! Brian loved flying. He felt the wind rushing past.

He felt the power in his wings as he soared higher, close to the clouds. He felt so free. He felt so wonderful.

He felt so grown up, now that he was starting to fly like his Momma and Poppa and his brothers and sisters before him. With wings spread out as far as they would go, fanned out to display the glorious colours of each individual feather, he glided.

It was then that it happened: Wanting to go higher, he raised his wings high above his head with all his strength - a beautiful sight to see - when suddenly there was the greatest bang and the loudest and most thunderous noise.

All the other birds looked on in shock and horror. Brian himself was so alarmed and frightened that he began to lose control. He could hear his heart beating louder and faster. Like a drumbeat in his ear - ba boom, ba boom, ba boom. He was so scared that he forgot to use his wings.

So it was that he suddenly began to spiral down towards the ground. Poppa bird immediately lifted off (once he had recovered from the shock) and tried to save poor Brian. But to no avail.

Nothing could help him. Nothing.

He went crashing to the ground with an awful thump and an awful bump, hurting his right wing in the fall. Shocked, his Momma bounded over to where he lay, bruised on the ground.

"Brian, oh Brian! Are you alright? Speak to me! Speak to me!", shrieked his Momma.

Brian shook his dazed head, ruffled his feathers, pulled in his wings and straightened himself up. He blinked his baby blue eyes and looked at his mother's face searching for a look of pride. Can you imagine how dumbfounded he was to see the look of horror on her face!

"Erm... well. How did I do, Momma?", he asked.

His Poppa came up behind his Momma and, peering at him closely, said in a sharp tone: "We'll not talk about this until we get you back in the nest!"

Brian hadn't a clue what was happening. Anyway, his head now as well as his wing hurt awfully after the fall - along with his pride. His could see his other brothers and sisters beginning to gather in a huddle behind his Momma and Poppa. They had started to giggle, even snigger, among themselves. They were also throwing him very funny looks. And they were not nice funny looks.

“What’s happening? What just happened?”, muttered Brian to himself in a very confused state.

"Don't worry", said Poppa. " My first time didn't go great either", he remarked. Diplomacy was never his strongest skill. "Hop up here onto my back and we will go home. Tomorrow will be a better day, no doubt".

And with that, they all went home ... somehow. Brian was carried home by his father. Some of his brothers and sisters, having tasted the feeling of flying, tried again and actually managed to fly high enough to land on a branch near the nest. They walked the rest of the way home, finally hopping happily and with pride back into the nest.

Morning broke the next day, and once again it was a fine day. The sun kissed the top of the trees and its rays danced through the leaves and branches.

Once again Momma and Poppa pigeon lined up their offspring to practice flying. This time, they decided to let Brian go first. They hoped that this might prevent what happened the day before from happening again.

Mustering all his courage, Brian moved to the edge of the nest. Momma was waiting for him below, cooing and clucking to him encouragingly.

He spread out his great wings, took a mighty leap and once again felt that wonderful feeling of the wind rushing up under his feathers.

He soared high, then higher and higher. Raising his wings above his head a little, he pushed downwards with all his might. With the earth fading below him he felt the tips of his two wings meet, and like two hands clapping with enormous energy, they once again made the loudest bang!

Such a loud bang! Such a shock! So unexpected! Crashing together like cymbals, the sound was like the loudest thunder you have ever heard in your life!

Worse still, the deafening noise echoed off the trees and rumbled throughout the woods. Animals on the ground fled for cover, in dread of approaching danger. Birds in the sky landed as quickly as they could on a branch of the nearest tree for safe haven. They all looked at each other, puzzled, for some clue as to what had just happened.

As with the day before, Brian himself was in such shock that he forgot to fly and once again plummeted, like stone out of the sky, all gracefulness completely forgotten, all elegance too. He hit the ground with a loud thud and a louder "Ouch!".

This time his parents reacted faster. They ordered him to jump up on his father's back and returned immediately to the nest. Poppa bird just glared at all the stunned animals and birds watching them. With a leap, he rose into the air to fly back to the nest.

Brian's brothers and sisters stayed put to practise with their Momma, and you could hear their chirping and Momma's cooing as each one flew and landed with ever improving flying skills.

Poor Brian, however, hung his head in shame. He had let his parents down.

In the days which followed, all attempts to fly resulted in the same disaster. Brian would try but darn it, there was nothing he could do to stop his wings banging together either above or below him with such a resounding crash – even when he didn't put much energy into his upswing or downswing.

People began to notice. How could they not? You could hear his wings flapping and booming anywhere in the woods.

Then one night, as the full moon shed a pale yellow light that lit up the woods, Brian suddenly awoke. He peeked over the side of the nest to see what had disturbed him. It was his parents cooing in very low tones on a branch some distance from the nest.

Brian couldn't quite make out what they were saying but he could hear his Momma chirping angrily back at his Poppa.

It was quite some argument they were having!

Worried, he tried to go back to his dreams but that night sleep was a long time coming.

The next morning, he understood what they had been discussing when his Poppa called him to come to the top part of the branch. This was behind a lot of leaves where the others couldn't see them.

"My son", said Poppa, "this is very difficult for me to say. In fact, horribly difficult, you see. But it is what it is. The neighbours have all been complaining about you.

They just don't want to have a pigeon that flaps so loudly in our district. It just causes too much disturbance in the neighbourhood. We have to ask you to leave home!" Dumbfounded, poor Brian didn't know what to say.

"Yes, we will help you build a nest in the roots of the tree. That way you won't need to fly around the place. Don't worry, at the start we will help you by bringing you food every now and then. But soon you will have to start finding your own way in life".

"I'm sorry, son, but you will have to leave home!"

On His Own Now

Leaving home at such an early age was a very hard thing to bear, made worse by the fact that none of the other animals or birds in the woods wanted him to fly.

And so it was that poor Brian spent all his days waddling through the undergrowth in the woods, putting one foot carefully in front of the other.

He would look up every now and then and see one of his brothers or sisters soaring high in the sky and feel so sad. He wanted to be up there with them too. But then he remembered his father's words: "No one wants a bird that flaps like you do in the neighbourhood".

Now, while it was great not to have brothers and sisters that quarrelled with you, being alone really was very lonely.

It was all the harder now because no one wanted to be his friend either.

Who wants to be the friend of a bird who isn't allowed to fly – because when he does, he puts the fear of God into everyone and everything in the woods? Well, no one.

On top of this, because he was so different, the others used to look at him sideways. Soon he heard them whispering the word "FLAPPY". He wasn't quite sure what they meant at the start. But soon enough, when they started to tease him and the whispers became taunts, he found out: This was their nickname for him.

Soon they were making fun of him openly and loudly, not caring an iota for his feelings. All so very hurtful ...

"Flappy, flaps!"

"Flapping Flappy flapped his way to the ground!"

"Hey! Say this tongue-twister three times: *Fickle Flappy frightened all his flock"*.

The taunts did not let up, and for Flappy the feeling of isolation grew.

He would look up from under the ferns at the base of the trees in the woods and see his brothers and sisters fly with skillful grace. He could also see the pride in the faces of his Momma and Poppa, who watched their offspring with such glee and delight.

But there was no place for him, he was not going to be included.

Oh, the world was such a very lonely place for Flappy.

The Princess of the Claddagh

Some months later, news came to the woods. It was about the daughter of the King of the Claddagh. She was known for her beauty and charm and everybody loved her. Her gentle and kind nature was known and respected throughout the city of Galway and beyond.

But one sad, sad day some evil dragons came to Galway City, and in one fell swoop they carried the beautiful young princess away.

Nobody could stop them. When they tried, the dragons would breathe out their deadly flames of fire and burn everything around them.

The people of Galway were devastated to see their beautiful princess being carried away by these harsh, warty and ugly dragons, off out over Galway Bay and flying into the sunset. The dragons moved very fast and soon all you could see were faint dots in the sky.

Wringing their hands in desperation, the people considered what to do. But what could be done?

They called out the army who, in turn, called out the navy with their vessels. They were ready to do anything they could do to save the princess.

Even local fishermen and boat owners set sail to follow the dirty dragons.

It soon became very clear that the bad dragons had landed on Inis Oir, one of the smaller of the Aran Islands. The princess was being kept in an ancient fort.

There, they defended the island from all who tried to save her. Many boats were burned or simply torched in the fiery furnace of the dragons' breath.

The days passed. Plans were made. Teams were put together. More boats were brought in – but success remained out of reach – the princess was firmly in the grasp of the dragons.

They tried arrows. They tried bombs. They tried nets.

Even the dolphins in Galway Bay tried – but nobody was successful. The birds tried – but what chance did they have when even the navy's ships couldn't break through? Nothing worked. The dragons would just burn their way out of danger. And so it was that the poor sweet princess could not be freed. The people of Galway, especially the King of the Claddagh, fell into despair

The news of the heartbreak spread far and wide. Even Flappy got to know about it in Merlin Woods when he overheard some of the other animals talking about it.

One day when he was feeling very down in the dumps Flappy decided to fly out to see for himself what was happening. Maybe he could do something to help. No one really cared what he did anyway – he had nothing to lose.

And so it was that Flappy spread his huge, long wings and set off towards the west where the islands lay.

At first, he took care not to flap his wings too much. That way they didn't bang about as much and no one would notice his departure and that he was actually flying again. He rose up and up until he was high in the sky. From there, he sailed a lot of the way, gliding on the warm sea breezes.

However, not being that used to flying – remember, he was only allowed to walk or hop around in the woods – he soon got tired. It was exhausting flying so far, and he realised there was no hope of reaching the island if he didn't put all his strength into his wings.

Encouraged by this thought, Flappy pushed down his wings with all his might only to swing them back up over his body just as powerfully. You can guess what happened!

His wings made the most almightily loud crash and bash, clang and bang. So loud in fact, that you could hear it all over Galway City, Galway Bay and the Aran islands! But more importantly, the dragons heard it.

They looked up with surprise – but couldn't see anything. Flappy was just a dot in the sky. They looked harder. They were confused and baffled, but they still couldn't see where the noise was coming from. What new danger is this, they wondered?

At this stage, the dragons stopped being curious and started to get nervous. Whatever was making that horrific noise was getting closer. The dragons began to be afraid in earnest.

Bang, crash, boom. Thunderous noises were heard ...

They huddled together for safety. Surely this noise could not come from such a small bird. Surely not? But as the dot in the sky came closer, the hullabaloo got louder and ever more frightening.

"Oh!", said one of the dragons. "I think this bird has special powers. If he can make such noises with his wings, what other magical powers does he possess?"

"Yes", agreed the other dragons. "This is indeed a strange and terrifying creature".

"I think", said the elder dragon, "that we should flee for our lives!"

Flappy got the surprise of his life to see the fierce dragons suddenly take to the air in a flurry and set off hastily in the opposite direction - they headed westward towards the next parish, New York.

They were quite obviously in a rush to get away from something that terrified them. Flappy looked behind him to see what it could be. But there was nothing there. When he looked down, however, what he did see was the beautiful princess, now standing on her own, freed from the fort, waving up at him, and jumping up and down in excitement.

Being a little tired he decided to land on the island and take some rest. He stretched out his legs to land and glided down to the ground. All at once he was being hugged. Two arms were flung around his neck around his neck and thousands of kisses were planted on his cheeks. And when he looked to see, he saw it was the beautiful princess!

"Oh, my hero", she said, "You have saved me from those horrid dragons!"

And the Story Goes on

The princess and Flappy found a stick and some rope. Having tied the rope firmly to ends of the stick, he grasped the loop firmly with his two feet. She climbed up and sat on the stick, like you would on a swing, and they flew gently back to Galway where a crowd awaited them on Nimmo's Pier.

The King could not hug his daughter enough, nor could he stop thanking Flappy. He was so happy to have his one and only beautiful daughter back in his arms.

All the other birds circled in the air above the heads of the people in the crowd. They looked on in amazement - and this included Momma and Poppa pigeon. They came up to Flappy and said: "We are so sorry, Brian. We got it all wrong. We didn't realise it at the time".

Flappy hugged them close to his heart, the biggest smile ever on his face. Right there and then the King of the Claddagh awarded Flappy a hero's medal of honour for being one of the bravest birds he had ever encountered.

He also asked him to stay with the beautiful princess and be her constant protector.

So Flappy went to live with the princess.

From that day on, they were close companions.

They would go into town together, do gardening together, and they even ate their meals together - and all the time Flappy would sit on her gentle shoulder or in her outstetched hand.

They were the best of friends. But they had one special arrangement, which went like this: Flappy was not allowed to fly up to land on her shoulder. Instead, she would bend down and lift him up.

Eventually Flappy founded a family of his own and they all lived very happily with her from that day forward.

"Funny that!", he would often think to himself. "The very worst thing about me, the thing that made others laugh and call me names, was actually the best thing that ever happened to me! And all through the bullying, I never knew there was a hero in me, waiting to come out".

The next time you see a flock of pigeons, and they start to fly, listen for the ones which flap their wings the loudest.

They are probably the grandchildren of the hero bird, Flappy. Smile at them, because you know the story... and then, think of the hero inside you.

The End

Discussion Points

This little story will offer ideas on how bullying affects another and how utterly lonely a bullied person can feel.

You see, bullying can happen to anyone. It even happened to me!

Did you know too that parents can make mistakes and they don't know it? See how great it was when mine said sorry - apologies matter.

One thing is for sure, friends can be found in the strangest of places; one only needs to get out there and find them.

Also, bad phases can pass; good phases come too.

Most of all I want you to know, sometimes the worst trait we think we have can often be our greatest strength.

It is always worth it to rise to a challenge as happiness is often the result.

Never forget, our own special hero is inside each and every one of us.

Fun Facts About Pigeons

Life span: 3-5 years normally but can live to the age of 20

Size: 28-40 cm in length   Weight: 250-550 g

Habitat: Coastal regions, however feral pigeons have adapted well to humanised urban areas.

Range: Global, except Antarctica, the high Arctic and the Sahara Desert.

Pigeons are known for their outstanding navigational abilities. They use a range of skills, such as using the sun as a guide and an internal 'magnetic compass'.

They're really good at multitasking. They can problem-solve and make intelligent choices. They can find their way back to the nest from 2000km away.

Pigeons are highly sociable animals. They mate for life and both female and male pigeons share the caring for their young, called squabs.

Pigeons are incredibly complex and intelligent animals. They are one of only a small number of species to pass the 'mirror test' – a test of self-recognition. They can also recognise one person from another.

Pigeons have excellent hearing abilities.

Pigeons can fly at altitudes up to and beyond 1800m, and at an average speed of 125 kmh. The fastest recorded speed is 150 kmh.

Billa & Buster

A Circle of Kindness

Giving Up

It was so frosty that the leaves crunched when you stepped on them.

Do you know that feeling?

The pale blue and pink skies showed that night was closing in quickly. It was going to be another cold one. With the fading sun, the warmth was now leaving the air and the earth. Yet another cold, bitterly cold night.

Buster was miserable. He had tried eating snails, spiders, ants or the barks of the trees, but yuck, they were not quite his cup of tea.

His stomach had been rumbling for such a long time now that he was used to it. In fact, he couldn't remember when he had last had a meal. Tired, shivering and terribly hungry, he searched again for a safe place to lie down for the night. He just wanted to be out of the wind and the rain – even if just for a little while.

He had called for help as loudly as he could, several times already. He had whined for help, also as loudly as he could, but no one had responded. I guess it was too late at night, either that or nobody cared. They were now all at home in front of their warm fires, like his own family probably was.

Three days now! Three days since he was ditched out and had watched the tail lights of his family's car disappear in the distance.

Of course, at first he had tried to run after them but the leg he had hurt during the fall slowed him down. He had tried to follow, but when he came to the crossroads he didn't know which way they had gone. So he gave up.

He kept returning to the place he had last seen his family just in case they returned but all he heard was the distant hum of other people's cars on the motorway, all driving away. For a long, long time he had sat patiently and waited for them to come back. He found himself howling to the skies above ... but no one had come looking for him.

After some long time, he finally realised that a dog's worst nightmare had come true. His family had had enough of him!

The nights alone in these dark, strange woods had not gone well. He hadn’t found anywhere warm to bed down for the night. The strange noises and smells kept him awake. He often heard old leaves rustling under the trees but when he looked around, there was nothing to see.

The days hadn't been much better either. He couldn’t find anything to eat. He had even run up to a few people who were walking in the woods. All excited, he had jumped on them – just to show how friendly he was – only to be yelled at loudly and chased away.

I mean, who wants to know and hug a shabby looking dirty dog with no collar? Unwanted - and unloved.

He sat tight and asked himself over and over again What had gone wrong? Had he not worn that big red bow proudly enough on Christmas morning? Had he not tried to show how much he loved everyone by licking them every chance he got? Did he not show them how excited he was to be in a family of his own?

He did not mean to pee on the carpet with excitement! And honestly, he did not mean to chew the edge on the expensive leather couch, nor Momma's designer handbag. And the shoes? Well, they were just irresistible, made of lovely tasty leather, chewy like the nicest toffee you have ever eaten.

Why, oh why had his family left him here all alone. With no chance of knowing which direction to take to get home? Why had they driven to the outskirts of Galway city and simply dumped him like garbage at the edge of Merlin Woods?

Being Homeless

You know, everyone needs a place they can call home! They need people and a place to go which is theirs, a safe haven. A place to feel protected, where you can be yourself and unwind.

A place where you are accepted. A safe roof over your head. It is where you can stretch out your legs in front of a warm fire and be with people who care, with people you can show how much you care for them.

And what about playing ball? Isn’t that important? What about eating and being together in a family? But things don't often turn out that way, do they?
Buster curled up in a tight ball under some fallen branches in the woods and felt so horribly lonely. He felt unworthy, as if his dignity had gone with the tail lights of that car. Sighing, he closed his eyes. "Might as well try and sleep through this cold night," he thought to himself, as he buried his way deeper among the fallen leaves.

Friendship

It felt like morning, Buster stretched out his legs and opened his eyes. "Oh no!", he cried suddenly. "I have gone blind!"
He couldn’t see anything. I mean, absolutely nothing at all! He blinked and then blinked again. Yes, his eyes were open, but he couldn't see. Not see a thing! Had he really gone blind?
He blinked again, and this time he noticed a really strange smell. It was one he had never come across before.
His confusion grew, especially when he found he was so warm. Warmer than he had been for days. Suddenly afraid, he let out a whimpering howl.
Three pairs of eyes were looking out of the darkness at him. Three pairs of strange eyes. He blinked. They blinked. He blinked back, afraid to move a muscle.

He felt an arm go around his shoulders. He looked up and two more eyes appeared. Only, this time they were even bigger. But somehow that arm felt a safe and warm.

Where was he? He tried to run but bashed straight into a wall. He tried to run in the other direction but came up against another wall. Where on earth was he?

Then a soft voice said in the darkness: "Don't worry, you are safe here with us. Last night was just too cold to leave you outside. I had to bring you home to our sett ... to our home."

"But where am I? Why can't I see?" whimpered Buster.

The soft voice replied, "You are here with me and my three children in our nest."

"Oh!" said Buster, "but who are you?" He had stopped shaking now that he knew he was out of danger, or so he thought.

"My name is Billa," said the voice. "We have been watching you for the last couple of days. Last night you were so cold, I simply had to rescue you and bring you home to my lovely warm burrow."

It was then Buster vaguely remembered being caught by the scruff of his neck and being dragged a short distance. He thought he had dreamed it, that he was back with his own Momma on the farm.

"So that was real? Okay. But who are you? And I don't want to sound rude, but what's that funny smell?" said Buster.

"Okay, it is time to go outside so that he can get a good look at us," said Billa. She gave the three sets of eyes the order and they all started to move in one direction. Buster timidly followed the shuffling noises.

Soon he could see a patch of light in the distance and several large black shadows moving slowly in front of him towards that light. He could smell the fresh air and he could already feel his energy returning. Waves of relief washed over him. He wasn't blind. He wasn't captured, he could smell the fresh air – and these people did not want to eat him for lunch. In fact, they didn't seem to want to harm him at all!

Blinking at the bright light he turned to look at the rest of the eyes that had been staring at him. They belonged to big black and white monsters! He remembered someone saying something about badgers being in woods.

What now? Not knowing what to do, Buster smiled hopefully at them. And what do you know?

They smiled back.

Friends at Last

"Meet Beppa, Benno & Brad, my cubs. They will show you around," said Billa to Buster.

Thus began the first of many, many days where Buster played and felt at home, safe, warm, and most of all loved. Together with the three cubs, he romped and raced around every day in the woods. They played hide and seek and had many a laugh together. Sometimes Buster even felt he was a badger himself!

Mostly the little badger cubs won the game. They knew where all the other burrows were and where they could hide from Buster. Whenever he got close, they would jump out and surprise him. Oh, but the fun they had! Lots of laughing and happiness.

Mind you, Buster didn't care much for their diet. They ate nuts and seeds, sometimes acorns from the old oak trees. What they did enjoy was catching rabbits or frogs, or sometimes even mice, to bring them home for dinner. If all else failed, they had to eat snails, worms or even creepy crawlies. Every now and then, they all would gather up leaves and grass for the home they called the sett.

On those days, with the fresh leaves strewn on the floor, Buster enjoyed his new home more because it didn't smell so badly.

As the months passed, they had to dig wider tunnels as Buster was frequently getting stuck between the narrow walls.

He was growing really fast, especially as it was turning towards late summer and there was plenty to eat.

In fact, he was now nearly as big as Billa, the Momma badger. They had started to spend more time together and found lots of fun things to do. Sometimes they would disagree or fight, but then whoever was in the wrong always said sorry.

At other times, Billa would prepare a nice surprise for Buster (or the other way around), just something they knew would be appreciated. They just wanted to make each other happy, and their friendship continued to grow stronger.

Hunting for more food took up a great deal of time as everyone was growing so fast and eating more and more food. This they did together, which made the task easier. He knew now he had a home with a family of friends and that was a beautiful feeling.

Mrs Joyce

In those days, there was an elderly lady who lived in Shraid Mhuirlinne, near by the Merlin Woods. Her name was Nora Joyce but most people knew her as Batty Old Mrs. Joyce.

Once a wife and a mother, she now lived alone, ever since her husband passed away and her son moved to America.

She didn't care much for fancy clothes or fancy cars, she did, however, care ever so much for woods and the animals who lived there. They meant the world to her.

At times people were mean and taunted her about her untidy appearance and the plastic bags she often carried around with her, but little did they know.

She understood what it meant to be hungry and have no one to care for you. She had promised that she would do all she could to prevent this happening to her friends, the animals in the woods.

So with every extra cent she had, she would buy food for the animals and bring it to them in her plastic bags, for as long as she was able to. Her "little treats" she called them.

Getting older meant it was harder for her to move around, but she really did love to walk along the paths in the woods.

What she didn't want was for the animals in the forest to rely on her food, but she needed to know that they had something to eat.

She was so kind. She even brought seeds into the forest to scatter them so that new food would be more easily available. She also planted sunflower seeds, berry bushes, wild strawberries and other sources of food. Sometimes the squirrels would dig up and rebury her bulbs or seeds. She called them her helpful little gardeners.

She loved being in the forest where she could see the seasons changing. No one day was like the next.

Every day, there was something new to be seen, life in all its glory.

In the spring, she would see the little bright green buds opening on the trees and seedlings turning into plants, pushing up through the earth's crust to grow in the direction of the sun.

Sometimes she would find a shell of an egg and know that a new baby bird had been born. More and more birds could be heard calling out to each other. She would often hear mother birds calling out to their young, encouraging them to fly for the very first time.

In summer, she loved the light flickering through the leaves, the bright flowers growing in the woods where even the odd animal would bound across her pathway. She would listen to the sound of the verdant leaves swishing in the winds.

Sometimes the branches would creak a little under their own weight. There were weeds which had grown so tall that they were nearly taller than herself.

She felt vibrant life all around her.

And autumn, oh autumn. For her it was a season of colours, a time of gentleness, a last shot at glory for some plants before nature took its course and winter gripped the land, and with it the need of the animals to hibernate. She watched the green leaves turn to rusty red, brown and yellow and fall from the trees to blanket the ground, covering it in a warm leafy coat.

Winter she loved too, for winter held a promise of good times just around the corner. That was when the twigs left over from the summer were now no longer green and supple but had dried out and cracked underfoot. While she wandered through the woods, it never ceased to amaze her how, right underfoot below the surface of the earth, the seeds were slumbering, waiting for the moment to send out their roots and grow in all their splendour when spring came. Yes, indeed, the woods were a magnificent place to visit at any time of the year.

A Sense of Danger

It was on one of these days when Billa and Buster were hunting for food that they noticed two strange men. They had that air about them that said they were up to no good. Billa and Buster were strangely disturbed by their presence and stayed, watching them for a while, but then moved on in their search for food. On their journey, they heard a crunching of leaves. Someone was walking in their direction. Billa who had an even better sense of smell than Buster soon recognized the scent of Mrs. Joyce.

Joyfully, the two bounded over to her. She always came to the woods with food for the animals.

Every day, winter, spring, summer and autumn, she would leave little treats out for the birds and animals to make sure they had enough food. They were, as she had promised, protected from hunger.

Buster and Billa just knew she would have something for them too.
And to be sure, she had.

While Billa, a little bit shyer, remained behind, Buster bounced over to her and craned his neck to get the scratch she would always give him behind the ears. He loved that, almost as much as the food.

She bent down and stroked him, talking in sweet tones to him, as she always did.

"Hey Buster, no one come to give you a new home yet?" she asked. "What a shame! Such a lovely doggie."

With that, she reached into her bag and gave him a special bone she had kept specially for him from her dinner the night before.

Buster licked his lips and nabbed the bone quickly before Billa could get any ideas. But lo and behold, Billa had not been forgotten and there was one for her too. Billa and Buster thought how kind Mrs. Joyce was.

With that, Mrs. Joyce continued along her way, throwing extra seeds and nuts along the way, happy in her daily routine.

But something did not feel quite right to Buster and Billa.

Just something was niggling at them ... a sense of imminent danger? Billa and Buster went on their way, but that bad feeling stayed with them.

One look was enough for them to understand what the other was thinking (as friends do). They turned around and went down the path Mrs. Joyce had taken. Just in time too!

They heard the cries for help and started running. Realising it was Mrs. Joyce shouting for help out, they picked up the pace even more. They came up to a clearing and there, in the middle of the pathway, were Mrs. Joyce and the two men from before.

Protectors

They had grabbed Mrs. Joyce and were about to mug her and take all her money.

Billa and Buster ran to her defence, snarling and growling. The noise was deafening.

The men looked up in surprise. Shocked, they let go of Mrs. Joyce. She fell to the ground. Now separated from her two captors, she crawled away from them as fast as she could. Billa & Buster moved quickly between Mrs. Joyce and her muggers. Buster barked his loudest bark, Billa gave her throatiest growl, and both of them bared their teeth. It was a frightening sight.

The men, now terrified, turned to run but not before Buster got his teeth into the trouser bum of one of them and tore a big hole out of it.

You should have seen those two men run!

Long after, Billa and Buster would laugh as they remembered the events of the day. How those men ran.... bullies are really only cowards, aren't they?

And Finally

Soon, all the Galway Newspapers were reporting the story. The Galway Advertiser headline read: "Kindness speaks volumes!" The Connaught Tribune wrote: "A Circle of Kindness: Woman saved from mugging by animals she helps".

They wrote how the two men were quickly picked up by the police. Passerbys had noticed a man walking funnily with a suspicious hole in his trousers and knew it was him.

Billa and Buster remained friends forever. And Mrs. Joyce knew she would always be protected in her walks through the woods where she did her good deeds for the animals there.

Billa and Mrs. Joyce were forever angry at that family who bought Buster as a Christmas present and then, when the job of looking after him got too much, did the wicked thing of abandoning him, throwing him out like garbage.

Sometimes, Billa and Buster would wonder at how their friendship ever came about. They felt so happy in their friendship and in nurturing that friendship.

Looking out for each other and taking care of their relationship was a source of great joy. Even though they had their fights at times, they always made up and their friendship remains strong right to this very day.

As Buster later told his other friends "Billa was not the friendliest looking animal and yet she became my best friend. It only goes to show*: You should never judge a book by its cover*."

And he would always quickly add: "Don't ever forget: *kindness given, always returns*. So always try your best to be kind!"

The End

Discussion Points

While puppies can be such a lovely Christmas present, they are a responsibility for the rest of their lives.

Friendships need nurturing to grow and stay healthy.

Friends can come from the strangest of places.

Homelessness hurts.

Never judge the book by its cover.

Part of friendship is saying sorry.

The woods are a wonderful place to be. They are never the same on any two days.

It is good to be kind like Mrs. Joyce. Kindness given, always returns.

Kindness is a circle.

Fun Facts About Badgers

Badgers dig burrows with long tunnels and a large room for sleeping. They are clean animals. They go outside to poop and they line their sleeping rooms with clean grass or leaves.

Badgers don't hibernate during the winter, but they go into a deep sleep called torpor. During torpor, their body temperature and heart beat goes down. Badgers sleep for a day or two, wake up to eat, and sleep some more.

Badgers are shy, but they are also brave. They will fight animals much larger than themselves if frightened. Badgers can fight off foxes, dogs and even humans.

Badgers keep mice and other rodents under control so they are actually good.

Badgers are usually nocturnal. Some badgers live in colonies, or groups.

A male badger is called a boar, the female is a sow and the babies are cubs. Badgers live together in a group called a Cete.

Badgers live underground in what is called setts. These setts can be fairly long, even longer than 50 meters.

The Golden Key of Wisdom

A Journey into Teamwork

Introduction

Sit back and let me tell you a fascinating story I once heard about seven little squirrels who lived in Merlin Woods in Galway.

Now, as we know, if you have seven people together you are never going to get seven people the same. And so it was with these little friends of ours.

Hoss was the boss. She had a beautiful long mane of hair, a bit like a horse, which was where she got her name. Some said she even looked like a horse. Positive, elegant and gentle, the others always looked to her for guidance. She would prance ahead and organise the group to get the job done, cleanly and confidently.

Bogge got his name from being like and even looking like a bulldog. Tough and muscly, there was always something slightly aggressive about the way he talked and did things. He was the guy who could use his strength to shovel mountains of earth when looking for food. He would bark and snarl at the others rather than talk nicely. But he had a good heart, and it was just his nature.

Foxy, well, he was the sly one in the group. He was always trying to start trouble. Sly and cunning, he liked to say nasty things behind people's backs and cause fights. Foxy was always looking for ways to create back-biting and opportunities for intrigue in the group. The others learnt to repeat his whispered comments loudly to each other so there was no nasty gossip and hurtful misunderstandings.

The tall yellow squirrel was nicknamed **Graffy**. With her long neck, she just looked like a giraffe to the others. But Graffy was always a little arrogant, looked down on the others a bit and was generally somewhat of a know-it-all. There was no situation when she didn't have a quote of wisdom to offer. But with her head up in the clouds all the time, she often had accidents, falling from trees or just not getting her balance right.

And then there was **Talky**. You can easily guess why she got that name. Oh my goodness, she never stopped talking! Getting anywhere with Talky meant the others often had to interrupt her. To avoid those lengthy conversations, they had learnt to ask yes/no questions.

The fat little round squirrel who never spoke much and was always lying around was called **Hippo** by the others. He was so fat and round that he looked like a hippopotamus too! It was hard for Hoss or the others to get him moving or motivated to do anything. He was always looking for a soft bed to lie in and really didn't think much of what he could do to help out the group.

And lastly, there was sweet little **Deerie**. She got her name because she did look like and act like a baby deer. Quick to take fright and lacking in confidence, she never felt her opinions mattered.

She was the smallest, so quiet but a great little worker in the group. Hoss always tried to strengthen her confidence by showing her the things she did well and praising her for her correct ideas and the way she could solve problems.

So why is all this important? Well, just listen to what happened one weekend in autumn to our seven little friends and judge for yourself!

Preparing for Winter

"I knew it! I knew it!" Bogge snarled crossly, scratching the ground furiously with his paw. “They're not here! "

He had been there for some time trying to uncover the hoard of nuts and seeds they had buried there the week before – but they were gone!

"Keep digging!" said Hoss. "You’re doing a great job. We just have to keep going. Winter is nearly upon us and we need to get our food stores ready. If the nuts are gone, why don't you try over there," and he pointed to a different spot a bit further over to the right.

"I’m so tired!" interrupted Hippo, melting into a heap on the ground. "I need a rest". He nestled into a nice soft bed in the leaves that had been warmed by rays of sun coming through the branches.

Sly Foxy decided to chime in: "I think someone here has moved them and not told the rest of us". That familiar mischievousness glinted his eyes as he glared at the group.

"Well, I remember once hearing a story that my mother told about her dray – her gang – that their food was stolen by the birds and they couldn’t ..."

"Now, Talky", Hoss cut her off. "Back to work. We will just gather together as much as we can today".

“Yes!" said Graffy, who considered herself the wisest of the bunch. "After all: *tomorrow is a brand new day*". "That's right," said Deerie cheerfully. She trotted over quickly to the spot that Hoss had mentioned and began to sniff. Sure enough, she had soon found a treasure trove of food.

"Humph! Hoss the Boss!" Foxy muttered under his breath, hoping some of the others might hear him.

And so the squirrels continued to root and dig for nuts and acorns or tasty flower bulbs or even pine seeds. Luckily, it had been a nice enough summer so there was plenty to find. Foxy, Talky, Deerie, Hoss, Bogge, Graffy, and sometimes even Hippo, would gather up the food, dig up burrows and store their goodies there.

But one worry concerned them all: The stores they had already hidden. Sometimes the food would be where they had put it, but at other times there was nothing left! The darned birds or rats had got it all. The squirrels knew that the only solution was to move their stores around every now and then.

Of course, they would have a fair good nibble before they reburied the stuff – so more had to be found to replenish their stock.

Day in, day out, it was always the same story: Search for food, hide it, find the stores already laid down, dig them up and rebury them somewhere else – mindfully and very carefully, all done to survive the winter when food wasn't as readily available.

The funny thing was that they would forget sometimes. By the time they remembered, the seeds had sprouted and saplings and other plants had begun to grow.

Deerie thought this was so cute when she first came across it. She felt like a great little gardener planting these seeds and then seeing the new trees and shrubs come forth.

With winter on the way, however, they also needed to set up their nice warm nest for the cold nights. Hippo was worried he wouldn't have a warm bed, but he was too tired to help with the preparations – or so he said.

Building their nest was quite a job: they had to gather a great deal of dried grass and moss, along with twigs, both large and small.

They would weave these into fine, warm and insulated beds for themselves in the hollows of old trees deep in the woods.

Last year they had built their nest up in a hollow on a large branch, but that had been awfully windy.

At one stage, Graffy had fallen out of the nest in a gust of wind. But she bounced back laughing. Her bushy tail had broken her fall and helped her parachute to the ground.

So they all worked hard at getting the food stores and nest ready for the winter.

The Big Find

It was on one of these days that, while scratching away at a bed of leaves in the quest for food, Deerie let out a squeal of delight.

"Oh, wow! Have a look at this!" she cried.

Foxy was quick to run to her side. Deerie was never the loud one, so it was unusual for her to be so forceful.

" Look what I've found! I can't believe it.... ". In her two front paws, she held up a wonderful shiny golden key. Again she squealed in delight and wagged her tail in excitement at her find.

"Oh wow! Here, give it to me. I'll ... I'll mind that for you," said Foxy, holding out his hand for the key, the glint in his eye reappearing.

Bogge wasted no time in joining her. Graffy, too, strolled over, not wanting to rush and ruin her elegant gait.

"Stop right now!" growled Bogge. "Not so fast! What is it, Deerie? What did you find?" Bogge disliked Foxy and didn't trust him a whole lot either.

"I've found a golden key!" exclaimed Deerie. "Just here". She pointed to a spot on the ground and showed her prize to Bogge and Graffy, her face glowing with delight.

Graffy peered at the object for a while then stepped back and declared: "Oh, that is probably the Golden Key of Wisdom.

You know what they always say: *Wisdom is the master key for the treasures of life*".

"Here, let me look after it for you," said Foxy in another attempt to get around Deerie. Bogge bunched up his shoulders and turned his glare on Foxy. "I am warning you!" he growled.

"Oh, if you say so, Bulldog Bogge!" sneered Foxy, finally backing away but remaining close enough to see what was going on.

"Let me have a closer look," said Graffy, holding out her paw for the heavy shiny object. Deerie passed it to her.

"Yes. Yes, indeed. What a wondrous object it is! I have never seen anything so beautiful," she said.

Hoss and the others who had been busily going about their business noticed the commotion. They all came over to see why the others were huddling so close together.

All except Hippo of course who decided it was an ideal opportunity to relax while the others were all so busy. He stayed where he was, taking time out for himself.

You can imagine that their quest for provisions was now completely forgotten as they chattered excitedly about this wondrous find.

"Show me, show me. I think I recognize it," exclaimed Talky. "It was like this, my father once told me that ..."

"Oh, give us a break!" interrupted Bogge aggressively, as he turned to Hoss to ask: "What do you think, Hoss?"

Graffy handed the golden key to Hoss who turned it carefully around and around in her paws with a look of close concentration.

"Oh, I bet you want to keep it for yourself now," snarled Foxy.

"So now you think I want it for myself, Foxy?" Hoss turned to the rest of the group. "Hey everybody," he said, "do you think that would be something I would do?"

"No, Hoss!" came from all sides, "that's not what you would do".

Foxy just glared, defeated.

"Anyway," said Graffy. "Deerie is the proper owner. After all, *finders' keepers, losers' weepers!*"

"But I would like to share it with everyone here in our dray!" said sweet little Deerie, blushing.

"Argh, what use is it to anyone anyway?" snapped Bogge.

"Perhaps it is of use!" said Graffy. "Don't ever forget Deerie: *Never put the key to your happiness in someone else's pocket*. In this case, I think we should try to find the real owner and give it back. Now, wouldn't that be the right thing to do?"

They were all looking at the key, turning it this way and that way, measuring it up for size, checking it for signs of what kind of key it was when Talky piped up.

"Well, I do remember hearing a story about a key once. It was a magic key with special powers!"

Seeing as no one was interrupting her this time, she continued enthusiastically:

"Yes, and if I am not wrong, it looked just like that key - or so I am told. Gold, Beautiful. Shiny. With lovely designs on it".

Still, no one had bothered to interrupt her, so she decided to go on.

"It turns out it was a famous key. Some called it ...," she paused a moment in thought. “Yes, Graffy is right. It is called *The Golden Key of Wisdom*".

At this stage, they all gave her their full attention.

Hoss asked quickly, "The Golden Key of wisdom? What was it used for exactly?"

"I dunno ... I can't remember that bit of the story ... maybe it is a key to open... ah .... something ...," Talky stuttered.

"Oh great! Just great!" Bogge blustered.

"Well. Maybe it does open something," said Deerie quietly, "but I’m not sure what it could be".

"Well yes, seeing as how special it is, it must be for opening something so amazing," Hoss agreed.

"I think I know," Graffy stretched her long neck out further, to make herself even taller than the others. "In my humble opinion, this special key opens a door".

Annoyed, Bogge snapped at her: "Well it could just as easily open a lock on a chain".

Foxy, sensing strife, added: "Well, I think it could open a gate".

"Or a treasure chest," Deerie offered timidly.

Everyone gasped. Maybe Deerie was on to something?

"It doesn't matter," said Hippo who had finally moved closer to hear what was going on. "We will never find out."

"As they say; *every castle holds its secret treasure and its treasure secret*. Isn't there a castle at the other end of Merlin Woods?" exclaimed Graffy, completely ignoring Hippo.

"Yes," said Hoss talking excitedly, "the castle! Of course! We should go there. Not now, but we could start early tomorrow morning. Yes, let's all get up nice and early and go there. We might find some treasure".

In a state of excitement, they eagerly nodded their heads in agreement.

"Yeah, let's do it!" they chimed in unison.

"Then, that's agreed!" declared Hoss. "Let's get some sleep".

On Their Way

The next morning, they were all up early, bright-eyed and bushy-tailed. Well, all except Hippo who had decided he was once again way too tired.

Embarking on such a long journey meant they needed a plan.

"Yes indeed," said Graffy. "It is a well-known fact that *if you fail to plan, you might as well plan to fail*".

"True indeed," said Hoss. "I suggest we travel in a line. Bogge, you go first, then Foxy, followed by the rest of you and I will bring up the rear to make sure we are all okay".

"And will we find food along the way, or do we bring some?" asked Talky, keeping it amazingly short.

"Good idea," said Foxy, "let's take some juicy berries with us in case we don't find food," he said, for once being a helpful part of the group.

They all agreed and their mood was happy and eager in the sheer excitement at what they were about to do.

"Hold on one second," said Talky. "I was chatting with the birds this morning and I asked them for directions on how to get to the castle. They told me to go straight on and to keep the sun at our back."

"Okay," said Hoss. "We will get there faster if we travel on the ground.

But we must always keep an eye out for each other. We will travel in the undergrowth and avoid the main pathways where there might be a danger. Every hour we will stop for a break."

And with that, they collected provisions of juicy berries and set out on their journey, the sun's rays warming their backs and bushy tails and excitement putting a spring in their steps.

Danger Ahead

They travelled quickly and sure-footed through the undergrowth, bounding over the leaves on the ground and hopping over fallen branches.

Suddenly Bogge who was at the front stopped dead. He sniffed and sniffed again. The others came up behind him, wondering why he wasn't moving forward.

Then they all sniffed the scent.

It was a dog. They couldn't see it but they knew that dogs were big trouble.

"What should we do?" Bogge asked Hoss.

"We will have to climb up high in the trees. The dog can't follow us up there," said Hoss.

With that, they took to the nearest trees, sprinting up the trunks as high as they could.

Sure enough, the dog soon appeared. One big, black and very hungry dog. With his nose quivering in the air, he had caught the scent of deliciously juicy squirrels. But where were they? His head swivelled this way and that. Now he could have some tasty dinner, or so he thought.

Hoss motioned to the others to stay quiet. No chattering. No banging on the branches. And no movement at all.

Deerie kept looking at Hoss. She knew he would keep them all safe.

But then the worst thing possible happened!

Graffy, attempting as always trying to be graceful and elegant, lost her balance. She toppled from her safe place on the branches and, like last time, her bushy tail helped to break her fall. But nothing could prevent her landing with an awfully loud thud on the ground.

The dog picked up his ears. He had heard the thud too. He crouched, ready to bound over to where Graffy lay bruised and stunned on the ground.

What happened next stopped him in his tracks. The other squirrels leapt into action. Bogge first. He zoomed down the tree to where Graffy lay and turned to face the dog, snarling at him. He bared his teeth, he bunched up his paws and made boxing motions at the dog. Seeing this, Foxy and Talky hurried to his side.

Talky did her name proud by starting to chatter – and boy, could she chatter!

The dog stood, rooted to the spot and stunned by the noise she was making and the furiously gesturing squirrels. Foxy shook his tail wildly, and Bogge and Talky followed suit. They formed a barrier between the dog and poor Graffy who was still lying on the ground behind them.

The noise they made was deafening. They jumped about – in different directions – all waving their threatening fists at the dog.

Hoss shouted to Deerie to help him and they sped over to where Graffy lay and helped her up. They climbed up the crinkly bark of an old tree to reach a safe branch.

"We have her!" shouted Hoss "Run for safety, guys," he yelled at the three still fending off the dog.

With that, Bogge, Foxy, and Talky ran for cover, fleeing in different directions up the nearest trees they could find.

The dog looked on completely baffled. "Darn it!" he said to himself. "They got away! No nice tasty squirrel for me today!" Shaking himself, he moved off in a huff.

Safe at last, the squirrels gathered in the tallest tree where they all huddled together, glad of the security, but also glad of each other's company.

"Bogge, Foxy, Talky! Thank you so much," said Graffy. "You were amazing!"

"Yes," said Hoss, "you were all so brave!"

Bogge, Foxy, and Talky, still shivering from shock, smiled a little to themselves and then at each other. Bogge surprised himself by grinning at Foxy and saying "What you did back there Foxy was really great stuff."

Foxy grinned back shyly. "Yes, but you were there first," he said.

Obstacles to Surmount

Having eaten some of the juicy berries and rested a little, they continued their journey. True to what the birds had told them, they kept the sun at their back. And they kept in line as they navigated the terrain. It was tiring. Not even Talky was able to chatter away as she usually did. Suddenly Bogge came to a halt, so abruptly that the others bumped into him.

"What's up?", called Hoss from the back. "Why aren't we moving?" He moved up the line to where Bogge was standing.

It was dark as they were standing in the shadow of a long and very high wall.

"Oh no," said Graffy, "how on earth are we supposed to get over this wall?"

Talky who happened to be a skilful climber tried to scale the wall but its surface was simply too smooth. She kept losing her grip and falling. The simple truth was that if Talky couldn't manage it, no one could.

Still, Hoss gave it a go, but she couldn't manage it either. They all tried but to no avail. Surely, this couldn't be the end of their quest? Defeated by a huge wall?

Driven by the necessity of rising to this challenge for the group, Hoss raced along the wall to see if there was a break or a gap somewhere. There was none.

Bogge reversed several feet, lowered his head and charged at the wall. All he got for that was a big bump on his head. The wall did not magically give way.

Talky tried once more – but again no luck.

Defeated, they slumped to the ground. It was Deerie who suddenly noticed that Foxy was missing. As a matter of fact, she couldn't remember seeing him for some time.

"Hey," she cried, "where is Foxy?"

They stood up hastily and were just trying to decide what to do when they heard a rustle of leaves nearby. Someone or something was in a hurry and was coming right at them ... the dog again maybe?

Before they could make a move and seek cover, something burst into the clearing. Whoosh! It was Foxy - with a huge grin on his face.

"Hey, guys! Manage to solve the problem of the wall yet?" He was grinning from ear to ear. The others stared at him in amazement. What was he up to?

"C'mon," he said, "follow me. Quickly!"

Foxy twirled and sped off to where he had come from. The others hastened to follow him, bursting with curiosity.

Foxy came to a low branch of a tree. In a trice, he leapt up onto it, and he motioned for the others to follow him, which they did without hesitation.

He jumped nimbly from one branch to the next branch of a neighbouring tree. They followed. High up in a tree, they spotted a long branch hanging over the wall and trailing down to the ground on the other side.

"Oh, Foxy! You smart thing!" cried Deerie. "You have found a way for us to get over the wall. And there was me thinking you had taken off for home and left us".

"Great job!" cried Hoss and Bogge together. "Great job!"

Making their way hastily down the tree, they all ran along the branch overhanging the wall and down to the ground on the other side.

Foxy looked around and smiled proudly. He had managed to save the whole adventure. He was getting to like the way the others were looking at him now.

Graffy noticed this, lifted her head high and said to him in a kind voice: "*Anyone can try, but the best one to take down* a *wall is the one who put it up in the first place*. Keep it up Foxy. We love it!"

The Swamp

As you know, there can be a great deal of rain, wet and mud even before the winter. You often won't notice the muddier spots in the woods because they are covered by moss, which makes them look green and grassy.

The squirrels were making good progress on their journey when Bogge, who was still leading the way, noticed that they were heading straight for one of those dangerous mossy spots.

Now, he was quick enough to sidestep it, but Talky, who was hot on his heels, wasn't so lucky. She didn't notice the danger and down she went.

Bogge shouted a warning and managed to prevent the others from suffering the same fate. They all stood and stared at the frightening sight of Talky sinking into the ground.

With arms flailing, she cried out in terror: "Oh my goodness, heavens help me! What's this? What's happening?

Oh, my word. I'm sinking and can't get out. What should I do? Please help me. I remember my father once telling me ..."

"Shut up, Talky," yelled Bogge "stop wriggling. You will only be sucked in deeper".

"Yes, but... Yes, but ... Oh, what do I do? H-E-L-P!"

"Stop talking, Talky. Keep calm. We will get you out but we need you to help us. Floundering around will only make it worse," said Deerie who was very worried at this stage.

"Oh yes. Okay. Okay. Okay. I'll stop talking. Oh, Yes. Stop talking ... Oh, this is tough. But I AM TOUGHER!"

She breathed in deeply. Yes, she thought, definitely not in control of this situation but I can change the way I react. I will be calm". And calm is what she became.

Graffy and Foxy were quick to return, dragging a long stick behind them. Grasping one end, they pushed the stick towards Talky who was as quiet and collected as could be. She grabbed the stick with both paws and the others pulled from their end.

"Yes," she thought, "all I need to do is take it slowly, breathe and do the next thing right".

Slowly but surely and with great care, Hoss, Graffy, Bogge, and Foxy dragged her back out of the mud. Deerie stood by to encourage her and give her confidence. Talky kept quiet. She was concentrating on helping where she could, the closer she came to firm ground. Wow! You should have heard the cheering when they got her out. Hugging her was out of the question though as she was covered in muck.

Willing paws then helped clean her up to remove the heavy mud on her coat which would slow her down.

"Gosh, what great friends I have!" she thought out loud.

"Yes", said Graffy. "You were given this challenge to learn something”.

"I think so too", said Talky. "Stop talking and start doing!"

The Castle

The adventures had taken their toll. Tired, they rested for a while, ate some of the juicy berries, and chatted happily among themselves. Refreshed, they continued on their way. It wasn't long before the castle came into sight.

"Oh, hold on a minute," said Talky. She smiled at the others. "Unbelievable but I've been here before and in this castle is a *Sile Na Gig.*"

“A what?" asked Graffy, stunned. This was not something she had heard of, which was unusual for her. "A *Sile Na Gig* is a carving in the stone walls of castles that was put there by the owners. It depicts a woman who protects against evil and brings you luck! The history of Sile Na Gigs goes way back through the ages and was very important

"Wow. That's amazing, Talky. Who knows? Maybe if we find it, the secret of this key will be revealed", said Deerie, holding up the key she had kept safe.

"Well, let's stop the talk and get going," said Talky.

She, Graffy and Deerie were gone in a flash, with Hoss, Foxy, and Bogge bounding towards the castle hot on their tails.

Once there, they decided to split up into two groups, one group to check the castle inside and the other outside for some sign.

It wasn’t long before they all heard Graffy shout: "Found it!"

They ran to Graffy's side. What was it, they were wondering? Was it a lock on a chain, a gate or a chest?

None of these. Graffy had found a *Sile Na Gig*. On the south side of the castle embedded in the wall above a high window, there she was, the smallest Sile Na Gig in all Ireland.

"Humph! I thought you had found something that would take a key," Bogge said.

"Well, so much for a lock and chain?" snarled a hugely disappointed Foxy.

"Now, now," said Hoss. "We are all doing our best. We should all ..."

"Oh look," exclaimed Deerie, pointing to a stone right next to the *Sile Na Gig* carving.

A closer look revealed a large stone which, unlike the others, appeared somehow out of place, as if it could be moved.

"Maybe, just maybe, there is something behind that stone, something our key can open!" Deerie declared excitedly. She knew she was on to something.

Her enthusiasm was catching and they scaled up the wall to get to the stone. Being the strongest, Bogge, and Hoss put their full weight behind the stone – and it moved! First a little and then it slipped back more smoothly.

Hoss peered around the stone which revealed a large opening in the wall. "Whoop, whoop," she cried. A chest! I think I can see a big chest in the gloom".

They all got to one side of the stone and, with combined strength, pushed at the count of three. Small as they were, they were able to move the stone to one side and slip through the hole. Hoss reached in and gripped the handle on the end of the chest. With the help of Bogge, they slowly began to slide it out from behind the stone.

"My word, isn't it large!" said Graffy. "A treasure trove indeed".

With that they carefully moved the chest out and slowly made their way back down to the ground, taking care not to damage it on the way.

The Treasure Chest

With the chest now in their possession, they couldn't believe their luck or contain their excitement.

It was a beautiful chest with a curved lid and designs on the outside which mirrored the patterns on the key. There were paintings in gold on the chest.

They looked at it this way and that, from left to right, and then from above and below. Sheer curiosity as the lock was in plain view on the side of the chest.

"O...kay," said Hoss, with a tremor in his voice. "It is time to see if the key fits!"

Deerie approached the chest in awe. She was quite nervous, almost as if the chest would burn her somehow or give her an electric shock. She held up the key in wonder. It was a thrilling moment – they were about to know the secret they had come so far to discover.

She inserted the key – and it fitted!

"Ooooh!" they all let out a collective gasp.

"Turn it now," said Bogge, getting impatient. He would have opened it long ago.

"Take it easy," said Hoss.

So, Deerie took a deep breath and, with one last look at the others, began to turn the key. Clunk, the key turned in the lock. After years of not being used, the lock was stiff and rusty, and Deerie was having to put all her strength into turning that key. Suddenly it gave one final loud clack and the treasure chest lid creaked open of its own accord.

They all scrambled forward, almost falling over each other in their eagerness to see what was inside.

Deerie's face fell.

Foxy stepped back, his face grim.

Bogge sat in disbelief.

Graffy felt the tears running down her cheeks.

Talky turned away to hide his feelings.

Hoss stared in sheer disbelief.

The treasure chest was empty! There was NOTHING in it. No treasure, not even a small spider or two. They looked again, once more, just to be sure. Surely this couldn't be true? Had they missed something? Had someone else got there before them? Sadly, there was no mistake, and no hidden compartment either. They checked. Slumped in a huddle, defeated, tired and horribly disappointed, their gaze was riveted on the chest as if some magic would happen.

But nothing did. That darned treasure chest was empty!

"Now what?" said Graffy. For once she had nothing super smart to say.

The Real Treasure

They closed the chest and left it together with the key behind the large stone beside the *Sile Na Gig* and started off home. This time their footsteps were heavy and no one said a word, not one, not even Talky.

When they came to the mossy mud, they stopped for a while and remembered how they had all worked together so well to save Talky's life. It was noted by all that somehow Talky had changed for the better. That lifted their mood a little.

They continued on towards the huge challenge of the wall. There they remembered how Foxy had used his cunning and his wits to help them to overcome this great obstacle.

From then on, Foxy had ceased to be so devious and sly and was now considered a "good guy", even by Bogge. They came to the place where Graffy had been attacked by the dog. Bogge looked over at Foxy and gave him a warm smile. Graffy beamed at the two of them, ever so grateful that they had saved her from becoming the dog's dinner.

"You know what?" said Deerie suddenly.

"What?" said the others. They had realised some time ago that Deerie generally had something good to say.

So, when she saw that everyone was listening, Deerie spoke out with confidence.

"We left home in the morning, looking for gold and some real treasure. When we found this key, we thought it was the secret to something special. But you know what? We found our gold along the way".

"Hmmm, I sort of see what you mean. You are so right," said Hoss, thoughtfully.

"Bogge, you discovered that being aggressive is not really the answer and that you have the strength to protect others. Graffy, you learnt how others also have something worthwhile listening to. Foxy, you used your cunning to save us all, not just once but several times. Talky, you learnt to be part of the action rather than talking all the time. Deerie, you have found your voice and your confidence. And as for me, I now know I can be a good leader".

"Yes," they all agreed. "Discovering our strengths and finding the good in all of us is worth its weight in gold! If we had found gold, what on earth would we have done with it? Build a better nest? What we found was golden friendship. The treasure we looked for in Merlin Woods Castle wasn't what was important – it was what we learned on the journey itself.

The End

Discussion Points

Everyone is different.

You have to learn how best to get along with them.

A team can work better together once challenges are met and overcome.

True friendship is worth more than gold.

It can be so exciting finding the good in another person.

What do you think of Hippo?

What is at the end of every adventure?

Graffy's Quotes:

Tomorrow is a brand new day.

Wisdom is the master key for the treasures of life.

Never put the key to your happiness in someone else's pocket.

Every castle holds its secret treasure, & its treasure secret.

Fail to plan, plan to fail.

Anyone can try, but the best one to take down a wall is the one who put it up in the first place.

Fun Facts about Squirrels

Squirrels are known as the forest acrobats, bandits, gardeners and tricksters.

They feed on nuts, acorns, seeds, flower bulbs and roots, spruce and pine seeds as well as barks of trees.

They chirp, make chattering calls and flick their tails.

They use their trails when jumping for falling to keep their balance and as a parachute. They can fall from 30 meters’ height without hurting themselves.

They build their nests with dried grasses and moss, usually in the hollows of older tree trucks or larger branches.

Really clever creatures they learn to navigate obstacles and are good at finding solutions.

Squirrels have such a sensitive sense of smell; they can even smell food that is under 30 centimetres of snow.

They put on weight to stay warm in the winter.

They lose a quarter of their buried food to thieves, birds, rats or other squirrels.

When they are startled, upset or alarmed, they shake or wag their tails.

They protect their food stored by digging false holes - also by digging them up and reburying their food several times.

They don't dig up all their nuts and seeds which results in forest growth, thereby earning them their name as gardeners.

Emily & Tristan

How Friends Can Make a Difference

Emily the cat padded her way lightly and sure-footed through the Merlin woods. She was following followed the path that wound its way between the trees in an intricate fashion. She was on a mission to find some dinner and had heard this area was plentiful.

It was such a lovely day and the sun's rays lit the path in little dance between light and shadow as they filtered through the abundant, fresh leaves on the trees.

It was then that she heard a loud thump, followed by a muffled, loud "Oooooh" and then, a lot of stifled giggles. She swivelled her cat ears in the direction of where the sound had come from.

Gosh, I wonder what that was, she thought to herself. Her curiosity got the better of her and despite the saying "curiosity kills the cat", she decided to take a look anyway.

Following the sound, she soon came to a little opening between some large trees and what she saw made her gasp and take a step back.

There on the ground in the middle of a clearing with its wings widespread and its beak stuck firmly in the earth, was a large owl which had landed flat on its belly.

From a safe place behind a tree, Emily watched as the owl struggled to get back up. First of all, by shaking its head left and right to release its beak and then righting itself on its two feet.

Once it had ruffled out its feathers, it mustered up all its energy and flew back up onto the branch overhead. At least it tried to.

The funny thing was though, when the owl went to land it missed the branch and careened past it, back towards the ground again. At the last moment, however, the owl managed to swoop up and avoid crashing to the ground again.

It took two attempts for the owl to get back onto the branch – but even when it had landed, it nearly fell off again. It was so out of balance it couldn't sit normally. When he finally did settle back on the branch, the cat heard a tired "Oh well", and then, a really long sad sigh.

"Gosh," thought Emily the cat to herself "that owl sure is off balance. That's not normal." So she decided to change her path and avoid the owl. Surely in a different direction, there would be just as many juicy mice to be found.

So off she went on her merry way and founds loads of little mice. She brought one home for her house Momma and laid it at her feet in the kitchen. She had gone to such trouble to keep it alive – but Momma just screeched and yelled and jumped about the place. Poppa had to come, catch the mouse again and remove it from the house. Funny that, thought Emily. I really thought she would love my present. How very confusing humans can be.

All that day and throughout the night, what had happened with the owl never left her mind. So she decided to go and take another look for herself.

Bright and early the next morning, she slipped through the cat flap and set out to visit the woods again.

This morning she decided she had no time to visit the friendly neighbour who always had an extra cuddle for her and went straight to Merlin Woods instead. She found her way sure-footedly through the undergrowth and soon came to the place where it had all happened the day before.

There, upon the tree, just where she remembered, was the owl. She blinked twice because she couldn't believe what she was seeing. The owl had its eyes closed but was rocking to and fro. Backward and forwards – and with ever-increasing momentum ... until the inevitable happened again.

The poor owl was swaying so much it teetered and began to fall off the branch. Emily didn't know what to do as the poor owl fell forward off the branch and hit the ground with a loud thud.

Oooooh no, not again," said the owl.

"In the background, the cat could hear the stifled giggles just like the day before. The owl picked itself up, shook out its feathers and made repeated attempts to get back up on the branch. No different from yesterday.

"Gee," thought Emily. "This owl is definitely off-balance. He has something wrong with him. He really isn't normal at all."

She turned her back on the scene and walked off in the direction of home again. "Who cares with that! I don't want anything to do with it", she thought to herself.

Getting to Know Each Other

Do you know what? Once more, for the rest of the day and the entire night, all Emily could think of was that owl. Something was just not right and maybe, just maybe, she could do something to help. It was at least worth a try, wasn't it? "Let's see what can be done," she thought.

So, the next morning, she set off bright and early for the woods and the tree where the owl was. As she came closer, she heard that now familiar thud, followed by a disappointed "Ooooooh. Oh well," and the stifled giggles from the other animals close by.

This time, she shook her tail, straightened up her back and walked straight up to the owl lying on the ground.

"Em ... hello", she said, "Is there something I can do to help?"

The owl raised his head, opened one eye, stared at her and said: "Go away!". He then opened the other eye, glared at her, ruffled his feathers and made the usual attempts to get back up on the branch.

"My name is Emily!", she called out.

"So what?", snapped the owl.

"I couldn't help noticing you falling off your branch", said Emily.

"Well, fancy that. Stranger things have been known to happen", snorted back the disgruntled owl.

"Well, I would like to get to know you," said Emily. "What's your name?".

"Oh, go away", said the owl and closed both eyes again.

No matter what Emily said, she couldn't get him to talk to her. In the end, she gave up, turned her back on him and headed home again. But not without first catching a bigger mouse for her house Momma. Surely, she would be delighted with this fine bigger grey mouse running around the kitchen – or maybe the bathroom this time?

Trying Hard

Try as she might, Emily could not forget the owl, and so she returned the following day. Approaching the tree, she could see the owl beginning to teeter. Instead of standing back as she had the other times, this time she ran forward with her with her tail straight up in alarm, paws outstretched, just in time to help cushion the owl's fall before it hit the ground.

"OH!", said the owl, "I wasn't expecting that!" and he looked a bit confused. There was no thud and no stifled giggles to be heard. He had landed higgeldy piggledly on top of Emily.

"Hello," said Emily, a little shook up herself. "My name is Emily. What's yours?" and she smiled her sweetest and friendliest smile.

“Oh, go on then.” He said in a surly voice. “My name is Tristan. What do you want from me?”

“Well,” said Emily, “I would like to be your friend”.

“Why should I care”, said the owl. But even as was saying it, Emily could see a faint glimmer of warmth coming into Tristan’s eyes.

Still, he spread his wings and after his usual two or three attempts, made his way back to his perch on the branch. He peered back down at Emily and said: “Are you still here? Will you ever buzz off!”.

Emily had never met anyone so rude in all her life and with that, turned around and stormed off, the hair at the back of her neck standing straight up.

Deciding What to Do

Back home again, Emily was really angry. That was no way for anyone to treat her. Honestly! Who did this Tristan think he was?! Could he not smile back and answer nicely? Just show some manners. She was so mad that she needed some way to relieve her tension. Aha! The couch!

Rushing at it with a vengeance, she scratched down all the right of it. It certainly relieved some of her temper but she sure got into trouble when her house Momma saw it. Seriously, that woman should get a medal for screeching, she thought.

All because of that darned owl, she muttered to herself angrily!

But you know what? That dratted owl was so unfriendly and yet she couldn't just brush it all off. Maybe that's the way he was because he was so off-balance and not a normal sort of owl at all.

Who cares, thought Emily to herself. That owl is just trouble. No wonder he has no friends to help him out when he falls!

But then maybe he is that way because he hasn't got anyone who cares?

All that night, Emily's head spun from trying to work it all out and understand that owl, and more importantly what she should do about him.

Help him...no, forget him.... help him....no, forget him .... help...forget.... help.... forget....

Oh drat, thought Emily. I have to do something because I know that, if I were in his shoes, I would love someone to help me. That's it. That is my decision! He will probably be rude and mean and rotten, but I am going to show him I care because I do.

Finally, she was able to curl up in a ball and fall asleep. Decision made.

Softening his Fall

Next morning, she set off with a spring in her step. First, she visited her friendly neighbour who had some nice treats and an extra cuddle for her like he always did.

Then, she headed straight for Merlin Woods and the grumpy old owl.

Sure enough, as she drew closer to the spot where he lived, she heard that thump, “Ooooh”, stifled giggles and an “Oh, well”.

She was used to it by now, which made her all the more determined to break the cycle of events.

By the time she reached the spot, he had already managed to get himself back on his perch.

She called up a friendly hello and a “Hi, Tristan. How are you today?”.

He peered down at her. “It’s you again! Will you ever buzz off and leave me alone?”.

Naturally, Emily was hurt but she decided to ignore his bad manners. After all, he was just someone who needed to understand that other people were out there who would be a friend to him.

So she found a nice warm spot, settled herself and pretended to doze off for a while – but all the while keeping a watchful eye on Tristan, the owl.

She didn’t have to wait long and, as he toppled of his branch, she ran beneath the tree. He came down with a boing and not a thud this time, bouncing off her back and landing gently on the ground beside her.

“Eeeeeeeh,” he said. “Ooooooouffff," she said, sure that one of her famous nine lives had been used by that heavy weight falling on her. This time there were no giggles either but Emily – and Tristan – could see eyes peering out from behind bushes and branches, blinking in astonishment. Nothing like this had ever happened before.

Tristan was also a bit perplexed. Who was this nuisance of a cat doing something like this for him?
He decided to take a good look at her. She was really soft and actually had the cutest eyes that tilted up at the sides. Never mind that, he thought to himself, I need to get back on my perch. And with that, he straightened his feathers, spread his wings and took off.
Emily, for her part, was still a little out of breath but felt quite good inside. Somehow the sheer surprise of her generous act him had made him look at her properly and take her seriously. But she knew she would have to find a different way to soften his fall. After all, she only had eight lives left now.
So while Tristan fluffed out his feathers high up on his perch, Emily started to look around for old brown leaves on the ground. It was not long before she had enough for a nice big bundle. She heard a rustling noise behind her in the bushes and swung around only to see the branches of the bush return to their normal position. Someone was watching her, so she hissed out, quite angrily:
"Well, if you have so much time on your hands to be peaking at others through the bushes, why don't you come out to help!"
Of course, there was no reply, just the sound of feet scampering away in different directions.
"That's right" she screeched after them. "Laugh and snigger when he has an accident but don't do anything to help out", and she let out a loud hiss which echoed through the woods.

Her anger gave her loads of energy and she had that pile ready in a matter of minutes – just in time for Tristan's next fall off the tree. Can you imagine what happened next? She had built such a big pile of bouncy leaves that when he did fall he bounced back up again, as if he was on a trampoline.

Tristan, who had been expecting another painful fall onto the hard ground, got the surprise of his life – and what a lovely one, he thought, as he bounced back into the air.

He let out a big gleeful laugh, but shocked himself in doing so. He had truly forgotten what it felt like to have a good old laugh.

Emily, delighted at the success of her bright idea, stared and then joined in with the laughter. It was something really new to see Tristan laugh – even if it was only once.

Back on his perch, Tristan actually peeked back down at Emily with a small smile on his face. Satisfied for now, she made her way back home again, happy that she had done some good on this day.

She wasn't sure but she thought she heard Tristan whisper after her "Goodbye sweet Emily. Please come again". She turned back to see if he had spoken, but his eyes were closed and he had his grumpy face on again. This time, it was Emily saying "Oh well" as she continued on her journey home.

Lending an Understanding Ear

It was some days later when Emily decided to check to see how Tristan was doing. She had a couple of ideas about him that she thought she would try out. So off she set.

On the way, she met some of the other wood creatures.

In fact, one friendly squirrel, who was a bit of a Dearie, came up to her and told her how great it was to build that bundle of leaves under Tristan. It had helped him not get hurt as often from his frequent falls.

Mildly annoyed, Emily replied that it should have been done long ago and that the other creatures in the woods should help out more. She told the squirrel to tell the others she wanted them all to do something really nice for Tristan.

The squirrel went off on a mission and soon returned with some of the other creatures. They sat in a hushed huddle for some time while Emily explained her plan and then checked back with them that they all understood. When they nodded in unison, she left the group and made her way to visit Tristan.

They all scurried off on every direction, all filled with great purpose.

Emily came to the patch where Tristan's tree was. There he was, rocking backwards and forwards unsteadily. Emily waited until he dropped onto the bundle of leaves until she said hello.

Tristan looked up, surprised. "I thought you weren't coming back," he said.

"Oh, I have been busy," she replied. "So how have you been?"

"Oh, the same as always really," said Tristan. "But this bundle of leaves has helped such a lot. I don't get hurt nearly as much anymore." "

Well," said Emily. "I have an idea. Would you be so kind as to take a stroll with me? I want to show you something".

Tristan agreed and the two set off. Seeing an owl and a cat going for a walk together was a strange but sweet sight.

After walking some distance, Tristan stopped and turned to Emily.

"Little Emily" he said, "why do you come to visit me so often? I am not a fun person to be around. Even my own family have stopped visiting me because they find me so sad all the time".

"I guess," said Emily, "it is because I like you and want to be your friend. That is if you want me to be."

"Oh, well, I think you will get bored with me like the others do. Let's just go back home. I am not interested in seeing anything with you today", said Tristan rudely.

"No way," said Emily, "first of all, you are not boring and secondly, don't be so rude. I have something I want to show you – but it will take a little time to get there. Keep walking!".

"Humph," said Tristan, but nevertheless followed her orders.

After some time, they stopped up for some nuts and seeds. Emily even found some old crab apples for Tristan to eat. He really enjoyed them.

As hard as it was to admit, he was starting to feel better inside.

It was his first time eating crab apples and a big first that he had ever gone for a walk with a cat.

But how long would it take? He wanted to go back to sleep and be left alone. Emily would hear nothing of it and forwards they marched.

On and on they went, her careful, light footsteps alongside his flip-flapping footfall.

Emily started to ask him questions about his family, his favourite food, what his best birthday present ever was and more. And Tristan talked and talked, only a little at first but then, he got into the swing of it. Soon, Emily had no chance to ask any questions as Tristan was doing all the talking. So Emily just listened.

It must have been over an hour later when Tristan suddenly stopped with surprise. They weren't going anywhere far away ... they had returned right back to where his tree was! Emily had tricked him! She wasn't going to show him anything special. She had just dragged him around the woods walking for an hour. The thought angered him, and then, suddenly, he was overcome by great sadness. Had his new friend tricked him just to make a fool out of him?

He turned slowly to look at her and saw she was beaming, as if she had just found a big bowl of cream. Surprised, his eyes followed her pointing paw. His perch. It was all different now.

He looked but still couldn't grasp the new situation.

"Now", said Emily. "Now, try to fly back up onto your perch!" and delighted, she gave him an encouraging nudge. "While we were gone," she said, "all the other creatures built you a special perch. We hope you will like it".

Tristan was a bit stunned, confused even, but with a dash of excitement. Spreading his wings, he gave a mighty leap, a downward swing of his wings and up he went, expecting to have his usual trouble in landing.

But, he couldn't believe his eyes when he saw first-hand what the others had done for him!

It was unbelievable. It was stunning. It was brilliant.

A whole landing pad had been built by the squirrels and the badgers and the pigeons and the other creatures from the woods!

There was simply no way that he could miss landing on this perch. It was as wide and as long as three times the width of his wings.

He could land anywhere! He would be safe! There would be no more missing out on the perch when he was trying to land.

He wanted to say he didn't care. He wanted to say it was a stupid idea. He wanted to tell them all to go away. But he couldn't.

He was ever so grateful! When he walked over to the edge of his landing pad and peered down, he saw all the creatures of the woods looking up at him.

This time, they weren't laughing at him – but laughing with delight for him – and a very warm feeling came over his heart that made his eyes tear up.

He beamed a smile at Emily and flew back down to be at her side.

He turned to say thank you, but she just gave him a hug.

I can tell you, that evening there was no happier cat in all of Galway, indeed, all of Ireland...... and no happier owl.

In fact, there were a lot of happy wood creatures in Merlin Woods falling asleep, dreaming of the landing pad they had built that day.

Making a Difference

Some days later Tristan was looking out and finally saw his Emily making her gentle way towards him, down the winding paths in the woods.

When she arrived, he flew down to see her and she greeted him affectionately. Strange thing to behold, I can tell you, a cat behaving in this way with an owl, but they were best friends now.

Emily asked him how he was and when he replied, she listened carefully. In times like these, she knew she should just let him talk.

It was time someone showed him he was understood and that he had feelings too, she thought. He described how embarrassed his family

was because he was always off balance and wasn't normal, like all the other owls. The expression on his face was so sad that that Emily suggested they go for a walk together. So together they made their way along the hedges and paths down to a different part of the woods.

Of course, Emily knew what she was doing! She had got to know this place a good while ago, mainly because her fur kept getting caught in the briars. She didn't much like the place but for Tristan it was ideal. There in front of them were the largest blackberry bushes with a carpet of blackberries on them.

Of course, Tristan had never seen these blackberry hedges before. He just wasn't one to go out exploring new places like that. He had never tasted a blackberry either, can you imagine that!

His face when he first tasted one big black juicy blackberry was a picture to see. Emily laughed out loud to see his bewildered face all spattered with dark purple spots of blackberry juice. Tristan couldn't get enough of them!

"Take it easy," said Emily. "If you eat too many, you might get a stomach ache.

And anyway, now you know where they are, you can always come back for more!"

They picnicked for a while more and then decided to walk back home again. On the way, Emily asked Tristan why he had never tried crab apples or blackberries before.

He explained that he just never had the energy to fly off and look for them. But since he wasn't hurting himself as often anymore and landing back on his perch wasn't a problem anymore, maybe now he would.

"Yes," said Emily. "I think it would be a great idea to start flying a little further away from your perch to see what else is out there".

"Well, now I think I could try Emily," said Tristan smiling at her, "but before you came, I just didn't have any motivation to do these things".

"You know," she said "A good old fly around the place could lift your mood and help you to handle being sad all the time. On top of that, eating better and a variety of food will help you too".

True, thought Tristan, but started to feel very apprehensive. It takes a while for things to change.

"Don't worry," said Emily. "Take your time – all you can do is try. One flight every day and better food. Just see how it works for you!".

With that, they made their way back to his landing pad and Emily made her way home.

New Routines

Over the next months, Emily would visit Tristan every single day. They would have great chats.

Tristan looked forward to these hours with Emily as being the most special part of the day for him. Emily felt that way too as she got to talk what mattered to her as well.

She told Tristan that she really did not like her house Momma, but did like the neighbour who always had those extra treats. She talked about the stupid Jack Russell terrier that always barked his head off when she went to cross over his garden. Tristan was also a really good listener.

He was also doing a lot to change his routines. He was eating better food, his day was better set up, he got regular exercise and now could sleep better, not all the time like before, but when he was supposed to go to sleep. Most of all, he wasn't falling off the tree as much, which meant the world to him. There was no more pain from the fall and no more smarting from the other animals in the woods laughing at him. In fact, some of the other animals would come and stop by for a chat. That was really nice now too.

Some days though, he still didn't feel up to much but those days were becoming rarer and rarer.

Finally

One day, early in spring, Emily went to visit Tristan. Something was different this time, very different: She noticed that Tristan was not on his perch waiting for her as he always did. In fact, there was no sign of him anywhere!

She waited and waited but he didn't show up. It was late and still he didn't appear, and she decided to return home, really disappointed and more than a little worried.

The next day she returned, a little earlier this time. She couldn't wait around at home; she was so worried. Yet again, there was no sign of Tristan. This was weird, she thought, and she looked for the friendly squirrels to see if they had seen him. They hadn't.

Then one day, a pigeon landed outside Emily's home and cooed so loudly that Emily heard him. Puzzled by the commotion the bird was making, she went outside to have a look.

"Hey," she said. "What's up? Why are you making so much noise? Has Tristan turned up? Does anyone know where he is?"

"Oh yes," said the pigeon, really excitedly. "You need to come with me – but I won't tell you why!" and with that, he flew away.

Emily was more than a bit cross that he wouldn't say why, but all the more excited to hear Tristan was back. She decided not to wait around and ran as fast as her little legs could carry her.

Was it really that far, she thought, picking up the pace. Her heart was pounding with fear and anxiety. Why had Tristan disappeared? Was he alright? Where did he go to?

All these questions were swirling round in her head. She couldn't wait to see her friend.

Heart racing and very much out of breath, she rushed to where Tristan's landing pad was. Lo and behold, there he was, sitting on his usual perch, waiting for her.

"Oh, Tristan!" she cried. "Are you alright?" But she could see immediately, he was more than alright. He was beaming from ear to ear. He flew down quickly to her and wrapped his long and feathery wings around her.

"Oh," he said. "My dearest friend Emily. You are my guiding star. Last year when you first came here, I was unable to be happy. I was so sad all the time. So depressed. All last year, you have been my listening ear, my friend, my ally. And you didn't judge. You helped me learn to eat properly and to exercise every day. You encouraged me to go to new places and do new things. You helped me to set up a routine in my day and I started to sleep better."

"Yes, yes," said Emily crossly, "but I am so mad with you. Where did you go? You have been missing for two days. I know because I came here every day. No one knew where you were. Don't ever do that to me again. You have to know I care!"

“I know you care,” said Tristan. “That’s why I want you to be the first to know. Allow me to introduce you to Daisy, my girlfriend”.

With that, there was a flutter of wings and beautiful white feathers as the most stunning lady owl landed down beside the two of them. She looked at Tristan with adoring eyes and he looked back at her the same way.

“You see, Emily,” he said. "On one of the journeys I took going off to new places, thanks to you, I met Daisy and we have fallen in love. Now she is going to come and live with me. I will never be lonely again, now that we are going to start a little family of our own”.

You could have heard a pin drop in the woods. Emily was stunned. When suddenly, a huge cheer went up around the woods. All the creatures came to the patch between the trees where they stood and all wholeheartedly congratulated Tristan and welcomed Daisy to the group.

It was such a happy moment, especially for Emily. She remembered back to the first days meeting Tristan. Boy, was she glad that she had made the decision to try and be a friend and help him!

So now, when you see an owl flying over the woods and a cat following, just think, they might be the best of friends and remember how friends **can** make a difference.

The End

Discussion Points

When people are depressed they can be:

Hard to motivate. Feel sad all the time.

No smiles, don't want to play.

Have trouble sleeping or concentrating.

Are anxious, hopeless or helpless.

Can be irritable or restless.   Feel empty.

Lose their appetite.

What can help?

Proper sleep.

Regular exercise.

Good food.

No sugar!

Having listeners.

Feeling understood.

Having a routine to their day with regular meals.

With the right approach and the right help, a person can get recover from the illness called depression.

Fun Facts about Owls

There are around 200 different owl species.

Owls are active at night (nocturnal).

A group of owls is called a parliament.

Baby owls are called chicks.

Most owls hunt insects, small mammals and other birds.

Owls have powerful talons (claws) which help them catch and kill prey. Owls do not chew their food because they don't have teeth

Owls have large, very sensitive eyes and a flat face. Owls are farsighted, meaning they can't see things close to their eyes clearly and they can't move their eyes.

Owls can turn their heads as much as 270 degrees.

Owls are very quiet in flight compared to other birds of prey.

The colour of owl's feathers helps them blend into their environment (camouflage).

Owls have an excellent sense of hearing.

Barn owls are very beneficial for farmers because they can eat up to 1000 mice each year.

The Lifespan of owls is around 20 years.

The Listening Tree

Befriending Nature

Introduction

Super elegant and naturally graceful, she emerged from the car. Her slim leg appeared first and then she stepped out fully. Magnificently dressed, the crowd cheered and roared in delight. The band started to play, loud, happy music. Cameras clicked all over the place, television camera crews battled to get the best view of her.

She was finally back in Galway!

Eyre Square was dazzling in the sunshine. Flags were waving everywhere and anyone who didn't have a flag waved their arms around in sheer appreciation. Children were at the front so that everyone could get a look at this great woman, the heroine of Galway and world famous.

She inhaled deeply, savouring the soft air. She looked up and saw the seagulls flying overhead. Oh, finally home again! The feeling was unreal: So exciting and so beautiful. The cadets escorted her over to a stage that was specially set up for her homecoming, right beside Browne's window in Eyre Square.

She gracefully negotiated the steps, to be greeted by the President of Ireland waiting at the top. He shook her hand with both of his and introduced her to his wife. He went over to the microphone and started to talk to the huge crowds of Galway people who had come to welcome her home.

"Muintir Na nGaillimhe..." he started in the Irish language. “People of Galway...”

It was a bright and sunny day and everyone was cheering with delight. She looked around and was amazed. How did all of this come to pass? "Oh, how beautiful!" she thought and her mind began to wander. Slowly, a sweet smile came over her face as she remembered.

Way Back Then

She thought back to the day when the change in her life began.

She fondly recalled growing up in Renmore. The place was like a little village of its own, with a really strong community spirit, people looked out for each other and where kindness was the motto.

What goes around, comes around, was the general understanding. Kindness is a circle was what most neighbours believed.

When she was younger, she never felt her two older sisters believed in being kind. They were mean and she was never able to see eye to eye with them. They ratted on her, caused trouble, and she felt they never showed her much loyalty at all. They were the gang and she was the odd one out – and that was not just sometimes.

Some days it was unbearable. All she wanted to do was scream at them and chase after them with her meanest face to frighten them away.

Sometimes she did just that, which only got her into more trouble. Momma would come quickly, a floor brush in her hand like a weapon, to find out what the yelling was all about and to decide who needed a swipe of the brush most. With two voices being louder than one, she always lost and was swished out of the room, away from the other two, no matter how loudly she pleaded her innocence.

She remembered the day she decided, "That's it! I'm off. I am going to run away from home!"

She went upstairs to her bedroom and packed her favourite blue jumper, a pair of socks and the three euros and fifty-seven cents she had in her piggy bank. All of it went into her schoolbag having happily ditched all the schoolbooks.

Once downstairs, she took an apple and a banana from the kitchen to keep her going for a while – and then out she went, slamming the door loudly behind her, just to let everyone know how determined she was.

When she reached the end of the street, she stood for a second. Now, which way to go? Well, she had heard that the Dublin road leads to Dublin. Dublin was big and probably had lots of nicer families, so that sounded like the best idea. And off she headed.

When she got to the Dublin road, she wasn't too sure which way to go. Right or left? Left or right? She decided to go the way all the cars seemed to be going.

It took her a while to realise that she was going the wrong way – back into town. Nothing for it – she had to turn around and trudge all the way back, past the point where she had joined the Dublin road and then it was Dublin straight on after that. Surely?

After what felt like hours of walking, her feet hurt so much she decided it was time to take a little break. She was dying to eat that lovely apple anyway. But where to do this? She decided it would be best to hide in case someone saw her. She decided to head straight for Merlin Woods.

She was just passing the entrance to Merlin Park hospital when she thought: "Yes! That's where I'll go first – and then on to the Merlin Woods".

After following paths through the trees in the woods for a while, she came to one very large, old oak tree. It looked so solid, so strong, and it seemed like its branches were reaching out to welcome her.

At the base of the tree there were huge roots and between those roots were cushions of brown leaves, which looked soft and welcoming. Finding a perfect spot, she sat down with her back against the old oak, breathed a sigh of relief and took out her juicy

apple to eat. Munching her apple, she began to take in her surroundings. It was so lovely here at the base of this tree, she thought.

A slight breeze would make the leaves dance and the sun's rays would flicker through the branches and throw beautiful patterns of shadow and light on the ground.

Above her head, birds flew onto the tree, chirping and cooing, calling to others further away and then flying off with a new sense of purpose. Around her on the ground, there were carpets of emerald green moss, long swaying grass, sweet little buttercups, little purple flowers, tall weeds starting to flower and old, dried twigs lying around.

This world around her in a kaleidoscope of browns, greens, yellows, and greys was so peaceful. In the background, she could hear the hum of distant traffic and she thought of home. Surely by now someone from her family was missing her. But she didn't care. She wasn't going back. She'd teach them to treat her better. She would rest here for a while. After all, it was a warm, hazy, afternoon and she felt so safe. With her back against the tree, she felt the support of this old Irish oak tree and it comforted her. She felt; "Yes, I am in the right place, right now. Here I feel stronger!"

What an amazing feeling that was – little did she know then how long this would last in her lifetime.

Family

Suddenly a voice boomed out: "Little girl, isn't it time you made your way back home?"

"I'm never going back to that place," she heard herself say stubbornly, even before she opened her eyes. Now, instantly alert, she looked around in astonishment to see who was talking to her. But, do you know what? There was no one to be seen.

"Who's there?", she asked. "Who just spoke to me?".

The branches in the tree she was resting against started to shiver and shake and the deep booming voice said, "It's me. The tree you are leaning against".

She jumped up quickly and swung around. She rubbed her eyes to see better. Could this be true? A talking tree?

Immediately, the tree waved its branches at her again. "Yes, little girl. It's me. Tell me, why don't you want to go back to your family?".

"I'm done with them," she said. "They are all so mean to me and don't love me at all. I'm off to Dublin to find a better family".

She told him all about the mean things her sisters had done to her and how awful it felt always being in the wrong. The tree replied to her: "Well, how about you try to be the best person you can for seven days. If there is a fight, don't join in. Don't call anyone any names. Don't get mad, just walk away."

"Try doing or saying something nice to everyone in the family once a day. If they continue being nasty, tell them how you feel in a quiet voice. As they say *the first to shout in an argument is the one who is in the wrong*. If they don't stop, go to your Momma and tell her in a quiet voice how much you are trying and how you feel. Ask her for help".

"Why should I!" blurted out the little girl.

"Well now," said the old tree. "See that twig on the ground beside you? Take it up and bend it until it breaks".

Puzzled the little girl did just that. The twig snapped easily.

"Now", said the tree. "Collect a bundle of twigs and bend them until they break".

The little girl did just that. She bundled the twigs together. No matter how much squeezing and twisting and energy she put into it, she just couldn't break the bundle of twigs. It was amazing.

"See!", said the tree. "That is what family is all about. One person alone can be easily hurt and broken. But in a family that sticks together, it is harder to break them.

Little girl, go home to your family and be strong with them together."

"I'll think about it!" she said stubbornly and rested back against the tree.

"Look!" said the tree. "The way I see it you have three choices in life. Give up, give in or give it all you got!"

But sure enough, as the cool night closed in and strange noises were heard in the woods, she decided that perhaps the tree was right. Maybe, giving her family one more chance might be a very good idea instead of trying to find her way to Dublin.

The place didn't seem all that enticing any more, especially as it felt like it was on the other side of the world. Anyway, her stomach started rumbling and hunger was kicking in.

As she made her way home, all she could think about was what the tree had told her. She was going to give it all she got.

Learning From Nature

It was sometime later that the little girl decided to take a walk to Merlin Woods. Now, with hindsight, she wasn't sure whether her conversation with the tree had, in fact, taken place at all or whether it had just been a dream.

She hadn't told anyone about it because they would surely call her crazy. I mean, who has ever heard of a talking tree? It was really puzzling her now, so she decided to check it out and visit the tree again.

Now, finding the tree again was no easy feat. They all looked more or less the same, and the woods change every day anyway, which made her search more difficult. But sure enough, after a while she found it. At least it looked like her tree. There it stood in all its glory.

She looked up and down the long trunk of the tree in wonderment, the patterns on its bark, its trunk standing so strong and sturdy.

Had this tree really listened to her and then spoken with her? It couldn't have, could it?

"Hello?", she cried out as she placed her palm up against the cool bark of the tree. "Are you there?"

Nothing but silence.

"Hello?" she asked again. "Are you the tree that talked to me?"

Silence again.

"Would you please talk to me again?"

Still there was no reply. Puzzled, and a bit stumped she sat down with her back resting up against the tree, like the first time. It was so beautiful here she thought to herself. The peace, the quiet and the feeling of being close to nature.

She took a deep breath, closed her eyes and listened to the beautiful songs of the birds singing higher up in the trees.

Some less beautiful than others perhaps, but then, she thought, if only the most beautiful birds would sing, then the woods would be a very quiet place.

Suddenly a voice boomed out: "Hello, little girl! And how are you today?"

Her eyes flew open and she jumped up in delight. Oh, it's true, she thought, the tree did speak to me. I wasn't going bat-crazy.

She threw her arms around the trunk as far as they would go and pressed her cheek right against the trunk, and gave the tree a delighted hug. The tree shivered his branches in delight too.

Stepping back, she looked up at him and said:

"I had really begun to doubt whether spoke to me last time! So I had to come back to find out. You know, I don't even know your name! I never even told you my name. What you told me to do last time helped me so much. I don't fight half as much with my sisters now. My mom thinks I have become a really good child too. Did you know I won't be running away from home ever again? And I don't want to go to Dublin now? May I please ask you about school……."

"Whoah!", interrupted the tree. "Hold on little girl. One thing at a time. Firstly, yes, I do talk – but only to special people who want to hear what I have to say. My name is Malachy. What is yours?"

"My name is Johanna", she replied.

"Well, Johanna? How have you been getting on since I saw you last?" enquired Malachy.

She sat down and told him at length how hard she had tried. Sometimes it had made her angry when her sisters still had been mean to her but she had continued to follow his advice, determined to make things better.

"Yes", said Malachy. *"It can take time and energy to crack a hard nut"*. In my experience, *"only when an apple is ripe, will it fall"*.

"Oh definitely!" said Johanna. "My dad encouraged me a lot, he said to me how good I was becoming. I was chuffed how he noticed. He praised me and told me how words matter so much; after all, so he said, *"it is often a person's mouth that ended up breaking their nose".* We laughed about that together".

The tree chuckled too. He chuckled so much that a whole pile of leaves came down on her like a shower.

"So true. Words, once spoken, can never be taken back. That's so important to know if you spread lies about someone. Lies can travel so fast, from one person to another. You can never take them back. It is like shaking out a pillowcase full of feathers at the top of a mountain on a windy day. Do you think you would ever be able to gather up every single feather again?"

"No, I guess not", said the little girl.

"No, you can never find all the feathers because you will never know where they have gone – or how far", replied the tree. "It's the same with lies, rumours, and gossip".

"You know what?" said the little girl "I never thought of it that way. I don't think I will ever tell a lie about anyone again".

"Good idea! You see, if you tell the truth, and people know this, it makes life easier.

When you need people to believe in you, they will. It just makes life a whole lot easier, not having to explain away lies. And believe me, *"there is no road in life without a turning"*.

Life can change in an instant. There will be times when you will need people to know what you are saying is true and believe in you."

"And, Johanna", he continued. "While we are talking about this, do you know who the person is that someone lies to most of all?"

"No, who?" asked the little girl.

"Probably themselves! Did you ever pretend something was okay when it wasn't? That is lying to yourself. Did you ever make up excuses for bad behaviour or why you don't do something you know you should? That's lying to yourself. Little girl, just try always be very honest – and most of all, honest with yourself!"

"Two favourite old Irish sayings are:" said Malachy. *"If someone shows you who they are, believe them. And if someone comes to you with a story, they are always looking for two stories to go away with,"* said the tree wisely. "People who carry stories about others are gossips and are just as likely to tell stories about you.

If someone tells you a lie, then believe that they are liars. That is who they are.

If someone hurts you with mean words, then this is their nature. Believe me, they don't have your best interests at heart".

"Phew, that IS a lot to think about!" said Johanna, as she sat down, once again with her back up against the tree.

That day too, all the way home, she thought about what the tree had told her, as she skipped along happily.

How strange it is to have a tree as a friend and she smiled to herself.

Compassion

Sometime later, Johanna decided it was time to visit her friend Malachy again. Things were going well and she couldn't wait to tell him. She skipped along the pathways with a spring in her step as she got closer to her friend, the tree.

All of a sudden she heard some strange mutterings and sounds on the pathway ahead of her. A little scared now, she hid behind some bushes. Soon, she spied an old lady coming down the path in her direction, muttering away to herself and scattering seed.

She looked so dirty and unkempt, not at all pretty or clean. Johanna made up her mind to avoid her and wait in hiding until she was gone. Once sure, she emerged from behind the bushes and carried on her merry way, so eager for her chat with the tree.

When she got to where the old tree stood everything had changed.

Amazing, she thought to herself. Nothing ever stays the same in these woods.

She saw a few saplings growing, branches had come down, new pathways through the woods were being trodden and older ones were disappearing. New birds were joining their voices to the older birds singing, and she could see the fledglings learning to fly for the first time, while squirrels scurried about, always up for some adventure.

She sat down beside Malachy and closed her eyes just to listen to the sounds of peace in the woods.

A familiar voice called out: "Hello, my little friend! How are you today?".

She jumped up, all excited to tell the tree all her news, all that had gone on in the weeks since she had seen him last. He listened carefully and without interrupting.

Then she told him about having seen this old, dirty woman, a smelly baglady, on her way to see him.

She put her fingers to her nose while telling him, pulling her face to show her disgust.

"Gosh!" said the little girl, "she even looked smelly! A real Raggedy-Ann. Don't you think someone should tell her to tidy herself up!"

And for the very first time, Malachy got angry.

"My dear Johanna. That is so disrespectful", he reprimanded her, only to continue in a softer tone: "Remember, just like you, this old woman deserves respect. She is looking for some happiness for her life. She comes here every day and feeds the animals in the woods. Just like you, she is trying to avoid badness in her life. She is alone now since her husband died and her son left to go to America. She also has known sadness and loneliness and she often she feels despair.

At night she is alone with no one to care for her, no one to make her smile or no one to listen to her worries.

Just like you, she wants be someone special, just as you do, and give love too. She wants to be loved, just like you. She wants to give love, just like you.

Tell me this much, little girl. Do you like to be judged by others? Too fat, too thin, too tall, too small, too lazy, too smart, too stupid, too pretty, too ugly?"

"No, not at all," replied the little girl. She flopped to the ground and crossed her legs.

While she was sore at being reprimanded but when she thought about it, the tree was right. She had never thought of other people in this way. Who was she to judge?

Thoughts about her classmates came to her and how she treated them. Being honest, there was one girl in her class that she could show a little more kindness towards. Right, she decided, I will do that first thing tomorrow. I will ask her if I can be her buddy for the day.

Going home, each step she took was slow & thoughtful. She had learnt a great deal from the tree today.

Saying Sorry

Months later during the summer holidays from school, she visited her friend Malachy again. It was another sunny day and the woods had changed again: different flowers among the trees, little berries weighing down the branches, the luscious green of the grass the leaves a darker shade of green. Even the ground felt dry and hard. She stood in front of him and apologized for not having visited him in so long.

"My little friend," Malachy told her "Please, no apologies, it isn't necessary. If you couldn't be here, well, you couldn't be here."

"Oh, but saying sorry is showing good manners," she replied.

"It seems to me that lots of times we apologize when there is no need to, like when we haven't done something wrong. Notice that?"

She shook her head and looked puzzled.

"Don't get me wrong," he said. "It takes a great person to say sorry, to show that they understand they have done something that might hurt another person. But some people apologize all the time, often when there is no need. When your feelings are honest and above board, why apologize for them?

If you are feeling sad, depressed or anxious, why apologize for that?

That is simply how you feel, isn't it? When you are in need or you ask for help, why apologize? Equally, if you are trying to be a better person, why apologize for that? And do you know why not?"

"No, why?". She carried on, "because you are not doing anything wrong or hurting other peoples' feelings intentionally?"

"Exactly," said the old tree. "Saying sorry is so important – but only at the right times. Using it at the wrong times makes it meaningless."

She sat down and talked at length to the tree and the tree listened. She could tell him everything and she trusted him, her best friend.

Exam Stress

It wasn't until the following spring that she returned to Merlin Woods. Malachy was delighted to see her and he shivered his branches to show his pleasure.

"Little Johanna," He said to her softly. "You have grown so much since I last saw you, I can't call you little anymore, now can I! How are you?"

"Oh, I'm good, but I have been so busy", she explained. "This summer I have exams and I am working very hard to make sure I pass. I'm so worried, it even keeps me awake at night. Today I just couldn't concentrate. So I thought I would take a walk in the fresh air, down to see you."

"Oh forget that," said the tree. "*Worrying is like swaying on a rocking chair. You sure use up a lot of energy but at the end of the day, it gets you nowhere*!" and he chuckled.

"Consider: "*Never dread the winter until the snow is on the ground*". Often you shouldn't worry about things until they happen. Doing exams can be compared to standing on a weighing scales to see what weight you are. It's only a check to see how you are getting on. Just do your best, that's all you can do, isn't it?"

"I never thought of it that way", pondered Johanna.

"Yes, dear Johanna, every cloud has a silver lining. When things don't go the way you want remember: "*What is meant for you in life won't pass you by*". You just move on, knowing in full faith that you have done your best but your path is mapped down a different route."

"It's hard not to worry when everyone around you is talking about how stressed they feel and failing," said the young girl.

"There is a saying: "*You have to do your own growing, no matter how tall your father" was.* It means just do your own thing and leave the stressing up to the others. It is essential for you to find your own way. So, believe in yourself, Johanna, you can do this Remember the caterpillar who thought there was no more to life. Suddenly she changes into a butterfly and finds she can fly".

"Oh that's a beautiful thought", said Johanna.

"During exam times, just don't forget to drink plenty of water, eat, exercise and sleep well to keep your brain fresh. And always remember to answer the question that is being asked in an exam."

"I sure will. Phew, it all sounds so simple but it sure is hard work", said the young girl, closing her eyes to rest and think for a while. "But then, I guess it's better than wasting my time worrying. Just get up and get going."

With that, she leaped up and after a quick tree hug, headed off home with plenty to mull over.

Later that night, in bed, she thought over the wise words of the tree. Doing her best, she thought, not so bad. After all, that's all she can do, right?

Steps in life

So many times in years that followed, Johanna would make her way down to Merlin Woods to visit the old oak tree. Always he listened carefully and always, he gave her something to think of, a new approach, a new way of doing things, and frequently with a "get up and go" attitude.

He would listen to her problems, her thoughts, her deliberations and then carefully reply.

And so it was that the years passed happily for Johanna. But soon the time came for Johanna to leave Galway to go further afield.

She had grown from a girl into a young lady. The old tree, now slightly wizzened, was waiting patiently for her, as always. She sat and leant up against old tree's strong trunk. Closing her eyes, she breathed in deeply, fully aware of all the peaceful life on around her, both above and below the ground.

The tree shivered his delight in seeing her "Oh, Johanna", he said, "My beautiful young lady, how have you been? What's your news?"

She turned around to the tree and started to tell him all her news.

She told him about how she leaving Galway. Her bags were packed and her tickets were ready. She told him how excited she about what lay ahead – and that she wasn't going to worry. She winked at him when she said that.

Tears came to her eyes as she told him how she didn't know when she would be back or when she would ever see him again.

"Oh, my dear Johanna", he said, and as always, he wanted to give her his best advice.

"Never forget your friends. Friendships need nurturing like young plants. Without enough light, food, and water, (and the frequent laugh) they won't survive. So please return to me."

He asked her then to do one last thing - to climb up onto a branch he had lowered for her, which she did. Straightening up, he raised her high in the sky, like a queen.

"Now", he said. "Please remember this no matter where you are and what you are doing. Think of me and remember the way I will always bend during a storm before it breaks me.

Think of how important my roots are; they are my anchor in life, so remember your roots and who you are.

Remember always to stand tall; be proud of who you are and enjoy the view of what you have achieved. Never stop growing. Branch out and expand your mind with new ideas.

Be prepared to let go of dead wood; ideas or things or relationships that drag you down. Take on challenges. Just go out on a limb and reach for the sky."

With that, he lowered his branch again carefully and she slowly slid down to the ground. She was all choked up with tears. She hated goodbyes. So she hugged him and then turned away quickly. After a muffled "Goodbye Malachy!" she ran all the way home before someone could see her crying.

Finally

The crowd cheered as she took to the podium and adjusted the microphone to the right height.

Utter silence descended over the large crowd. You could have heard a pin drop.

"Muintir na nGaillimhe, people of Galway", she began. "I am here today, filled with joy and pride. Pride in my land and my country and most of all, in this fabulous, diverse city which I spent my childhood and formative years.

Certainly, I have seen and done a lot. Much of this has been widely covered in the media and on the internet. But, I would like to speak with you today, not about myself but our relationship with this earth. In particular, I ask you to imagine what would our lives be like if we had no trees. No trees! Unimaginable, right?

Trees are both beautiful and majestic and no two are alike. Trees are lovely to behold – but more importantly, they play such an important role in our world.

They help control our climate by reducing the negative effects of the sun, rain and wind. Their shade protects us from harmful ultraviolet rays, keeps us cool in summer and shelters us in winter from wind, sleet, rain and hail.

They filter our air and provide us with oxygen as well as conserve water, preserve soil, support wildlife and protect biodiversity.

Our birds make their homes in the trees, the bees that bring us honey and pollinate our flowers depend on trees, our insects that feed our birds and enrich our soil depend on trees. All of this would be gone, if we lost our trees.

My dear friends! We have only one mother earth. If we don't protect her, we will not have an earth to live on! Part of nurturing our environment is being a friend to nature.

And I know, with absolute certainty, that trees are our friends. So let us play our part! Let us plant more trees and nurture our friendships with them!"

As the crowd cheered their appreciation, she wondered to herself: Did the tree's advice help her become the success she was? She couldn't say for certain but following the ideas and advice he had given her had most assuredly made her life a whole lot easier.

And she smiled in love and appreciation.

The End

How Trees Are Our Friends

Trees protect biodiversity by providing habitats for birds, bees, insects and animals.

Children who play around trees are more relaxed and attentive which improves learning and performance in school.

Shade from trees reduce exposure to cancer-causing UV rays. Tree-lined streets encourage walking, helping meet daily exercise requirements

Trees promote healing and wellbeing. Trees lower blood pressure and improve heart rate.

Trees decrease mental fatigue and make people feel more peaceful, tranquil and restful. Trees help patients get better. Being near trees can improve coping skills and healing.

Food from trees are healthy to eat as they boost the immune system and increase healthy fats that reduce bad cholesterol.

Trees and shrubs can reduce stressful noises by 50%.

Trees produce oxygen and reduce smog. Trees take in carbon dioxide (CO2), reducing the overall concentration of greenhouse gases in the atmosphere.

Trees filter up to a third of fine particle pollutants in the air near the tree. Due to better air, trees reduce cardiac disease, strokes and asthma.

Old Irish Sayings

The first to shout in an argument is the one who is in the wrong.

Only when an apple is ripe, will it fall.

It is often a person's mouth that ended up breaking their nose.

There is no road in life without a turning.

If someone shows you who they are, believe them.

If someone comes to you with a story, they are always looking for two stories to go away with.

Never dread the winter until the snow is on the ground.

What is meant for you in life simply won't pass you by.

You have to do your own growing, no matter how tall your father was.

Acknowledgements

I would like to express my heartfelt thanks to

Fionn and Kealan, my sons who have been my helpers throughout all my writing and musings.

Diana Polkinghorne, my dear friend, who bravely proofread and edited all these stories.

Terry O Flaherty, who has been a constant and tremendous support as well as a kind friend.

Emily Deavy, a kind friend and guiding light; a star.

Liam Begley, my big brother who has been such a great help throughout.

Susanna Lobina, an incredible & inspiring sister-in-arms.

And to my friends, Eliza, Karina, Susanna, Anca, Ljudmila, Gelika, Cemile, Mandy, Edwina, Brian Vibenholt and Austin Donnelly

.

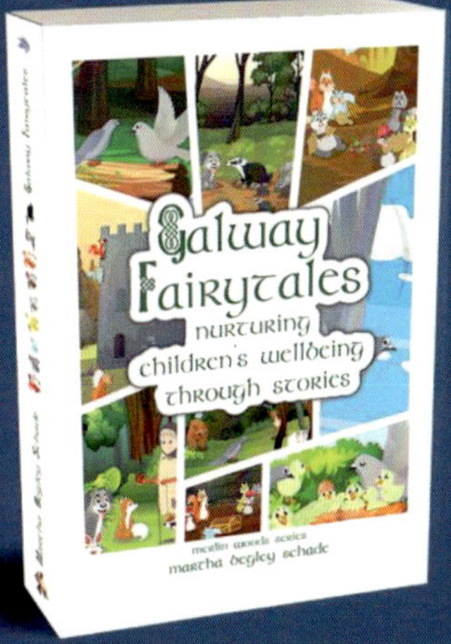

More by Martha

Social issues brought
to life in engaging tales,
sure to captivate
as well as educate.

Enjoy as individual books or
one big compliation book.

Join our friends in Merlin Woods for
more exciting adventures.

Ask me more at:
marthabegleybooks
@gmail.com

Martha